Love
The
Shoes!

FASHION

Tyndale House Publishers, Inc. Carol Stream, Illinois

# Through Thick & Thin

## Sandra Byrd

Visit Tyndale's exciting Web site at www.tyndale.com.

Visit Sandra Byrd's Web site at www.sandrabyrd.com.

*TYNDALE* and Tyndale's quill logo are registered trademarks of Tyndale House Publishers, Inc.

*Through Thick & Thin*

Designed by Jennifer Ghionzoli

Edited by Stephanie Voiland

Published in association with the literary agency of Browne & Miller Literary Associates, LLC, 410 Michigan Avenue, Suite 460, Chicago, IL 60605.

Unless otherwise indicated, all Scripture quotations are taken from the *Holy Bible*, New Living Translation, copyright © 1996, 2004, 2007 by Tyndale House Foundation. Used by permission of Tyndale House Publishers, Inc., Carol Stream, Illinois 60188. All rights reserved.

Scripture quotations marked NIV are taken from the *Holy Bible*, New International Version®, NIV®. Copyright © 1973, 1978, 1984 by Biblica, Inc.™ Used by permission of Zondervan. All rights reserved worldwide.

For manufacturing information regarding this product, please call 1-800-323-9400.

**Library of Congress Cataloging-in-Publication Data**

Byrd, Sandra.
    Through thick & thin / Sandra Byrd.
        p. cm. — (London confidential ; [#2])
    Summary: Fifteen-year-old Savvy Smith, an American living near London, sees her chance to write a full column for her school newspaper, and must rely on her Christian faith when she is forced to choose between friends, family, and fame.
    ISBN 978-1-4143-2598-9 (sc)
    [1. Schools—Fiction.  2. Advice columns—Fiction.  3. Americans—England—London—Fiction.  4. Fashion—Fiction.  5. Christian life—Fiction.  6. London (England)—Fiction.  7. England—Fiction.]  I. Title.  II. Title: Through thick and thin.

PZ7.B9898Thr 2010
[Fic]—dc22                                                              2009046892

Printed in the United States of America.

16  15  14  13  12  11  10
 7   6   5   4   3   2   1

**FOR DEBBIE AUSTIN:**

*friends through thick and thin for nearly twenty years*

# Chapter 1

It was ten minutes before I had to leave the house to get to my school, Wexburg Academy, the first day back after Christmas vacation. And my hair was a mess. I mean the kind of mess that you can't possibly show up to school with, not if you're fifteen and your hair is third in importance in your life. Right after God and family. Some days, right after God. Kidding!

I ditched the downstairs bathroom and slid into the kitchen. "I'm sick. I have to stay home," I told my mother as she wiped down the counter and put the toaster away. "I think it's the flu." I coughed three times for effect.

"You look fine to me," she said. My dad chugged down his normal breakfast of tomato

1

juice with a shot of hot pepper sauce, snorted, and glanced up.

"You look fine to me, too," he said. "New hairdo?"

"Yes. I call it 'running in a wind tunnel.' Or maybe 'standing too close to firecrackers.' Or 'I'd like to lose the tiny social standing I've gained in the six months we've lived here.'"

Here's a new rule for my fashion notebook: I will never, ever, ever attempt to scrunch my hair without washing it the day after I've flat-ironed it. Never.

And here's a second rule, one I should have known by now: don't ever try new hair products on a school day.

"You like different fashions, Savvy," my little sister, Louanne, said. "You're just setting a new style." Her dog, Giggle, who should have been named Growl, stared at me. I knew he was mocking me. I gave him the stink eye and promised myself to chase him with a running vacuum cleaner after school.

"I can't go, Mom. I really can't."

"You really can," she said as she looked at her watch. "In fact, you must. Better get a jacket on and head out."

"Why is *your* hair done so early, Mom?" Louanne asked. I pulled myself out of my panic-attack nosedive long enough to look at my mother. It was true. Her hair was done. And her makeup. And she had actual clothes on—not sweats.

"Vivienne asked me to come with her to check out some fund-raising ideas for the book club." She seemed pleased that she'd made a friend. Louanne had made some friends too. Even my dad had made a friend at work.

And *moi*? Not yet. Most of my friends back home had quietly slipped away as they became involved with their own activities. I'd had a couple of potential friends here at the end of the term, but one look at this do and it would be all over. With any luck, I wouldn't run into any of the populars—the Aristocats, as I called them—today.

I pulled a smart, stylish jacket over my school uniform. Too bad hats were only in for the tea-with-the-Queen set. I glanced at my hair in the hallway mirror. Worse than I'd remembered.

The walk to school was about ten minutes, and I pulled out my new schedule to review on the way there. This was term change, so it was mostly old classes and a few new ones. For one, second period was changing from health to PE. Everyone's hair would look bad after PE. Right?

First period was maths, as they say here in Britain. My archenemy on the newspaper staff, Hazelle, was in that class. So was Brian, a boy who had started out not liking me, but we'd bonded over a stick of gum. When I got to school, I slid into the seat next to him.

"How was Christmas?" he asked politely, never taking his eyes off my hair.

"I know; it's a disaster," I said. "Christmas was fine. Yours?"

"Fine," he said, not bothering to contradict me about the disastrous hair.

Hazelle walked in. "Hullo, Savvy," she said, setting down her book bag a few chairs away from mine. "New hairdo?" she asked with a snarky edge to her voice.

I bit back a few words about how her hairstyle could use any kind of shaping at all, and smiled. "Welcome back to school, Hazelle," I said sweetly. Even Mr. Thompson gave me a startled glance when he entered the room, but like any good Brit, he recovered his poker face rather quickly. I toughed it out through the class, knowing that PE was next and with it, hopefully some relief.

Afterward, people would probably just assume that my hair was the result of a really dedicated, energetic workout.

I picked up my book bag and headed for the gym. I walked into the changing room. And then I saw them, all propped up against the mirrored, stainless-steel countertops like a complete set of high-society British Barbies. They'd taken up every available plug for their hair gear. Oh, great.

The Aristocats.

# Chapter 2

Five faces with smirks on them, one face with a friendly but questioning expression. That would be Penny.

One of the others spoke up. "Look, it's Savannah, the newspaper delivery girl. Whatever happened to your hair?"

"I got caught in an electrical storm on the way to school," I answered as tartly as I could. I had to admit, the dismissive "newspaper delivery girl" comment hurt me even more than the hair critique. I wished I could tell them about my *real* role at the paper.

"A lot of top models wear their hair like that," Penny helpfully offered. "It's a carefree look."

I cast a grateful glance in her direction but went

to change into my PE uniform. I didn't want her to become guilty by association—with me. Thankfully, Gwennie and Jill, two girls from my science class, were also in PE, so I hung out with them.

"Don't worry about them." Gwennie nodded at the Aristocats. "They only know how to do their hair one way. Otherwise, they might forget how."

I grinned at her, appreciating her support. After volleyball we returned to the changing room, and I smiled at Penny, whom I'd met during an unsuccessful attempt to join the art club last term. She grinned back, not caring, it seemed, who among her clique was looking. Of course, they were all heads-down, texting, so maybe they didn't notice anyway.

And then, as if by a special gift from God, my own phone beeped to let me know a text was coming in. Two of the Aristocats looked up—shocked, I suppose, that I actually had friends. I grinned when I saw who it was and knew they'd be impressed if I told them, which I wouldn't, because *my* mother had taught me not to be the bragging type.

The text was from Union Jack, the supercute year-twelve editor of the school paper. It read:

Savvy—meet me in the courtyard before lunch, all right?

I couldn't believe it! Jack, the only other person on campus who knew my secret, was meeting with me privately.

Then I remembered my hair.

I gutted through third period, science, with Gwennie and Jill—obviously Best Friends with a capital *B* and a capital *F*. They were making plans for the week ahead . . . together. They were quiet about it—so I wouldn't feel left out, I suppose. Which was really nice of them. But I longed to have someone to make fun plans with too. My own capital *B*, capital *F* right here in my new hometown outside of London.

After third period, I raced to the courtyard to meet Jack. He looked just as good after the holidays as he had before—not that I was surprised! And he was just as nice, too.

"Hullo, Savvy," he said, flashing *that smile* at me. "Enjoy the holidays?"

I grinned. "Yes, I did."

"Brilliant," he said. "Listen, Savvy, I've got a handful of questions for the Asking for Trouble column. A whole bunch of them came in over the break—both by e-mail and stuck into the box outside the newspaper office. You're a sensation!"

I blushed, pleased to be acknowledged. Yes,

I was a hit—and that was great. But I was a *secret* hit. Last term I'd been chosen through a contest to be the writer for the Wexburg Academy *Times* advice column, giving advice on everyday problems submitted by students in our school. But my identity was to remain hidden. It had been my choice, and I believed it was the right one. Still, I sometimes wished people knew I wrote it. That I wasn't only, as the Aristocats thought, the paper delivery girl. That I was an *actual writer*.

I could picture it now. Their leader, who'd spoken out after gym class, would be kind of embarrassed. She'd apologize, and maybe even admit that she'd written in a question that I'd answered for her. An answer that had changed her life. I'd be humble and, of course, accept her invitation to sit with her group at lunch.

"Savvy!" Jack's voice snapped me out of my daydream and back to reality.

"Oh, uh, sorry."

"Right," he said, looking kind of annoyed. "Anyway, as I was saying, here are a stack of questions. They all work for me. Choose the ones you want, and make sure you get them to me by e-mail on Tuesday night before each publication. Okay? We're hoping to run the column each week except January 21. Special sports edition of the paper. Not too much writing for you, is it?" he asked.

"No, not at all," I said. "I'd love more, even!"

He grinned and headed back to the lunchroom, where I'd join him at the newspaper staff table shortly. I was allowed to sit there now. I was the paper delivery girl.

But I was hoping to be much, much more. I'd have to find a way to do that without blowing my cover.

Easy enough. Right?

# Chapter 3

After dinner that night I helped Louanne clean up the kitchen—my dad was working late and my mother was on the phone—again. Then I went up to my room to do my homework.

Not much homework, of course—first day back.

I strummed my guitar. Didn't want to get rusty. But I did it quietly so as not to set off Vivienne, our next-door neighbor.

I wrote an e-mail to Jen, my old best friend in Seattle. Didn't know if I'd hear back or not.

Then I pulled out the stack of questions that Jack had gathered over the break and began reading through them. When I first started doing these columns, I realized very quickly that this wasn't just about giving advice to other people. Somehow the Lord used every question I answered to teach *me* something too. I wasn't exactly happy about that. But I guess it's only fair. After all, how could I go spouting off on something I knew nothing about? I couldn't say it didn't influence the questions I chose, though, because I didn't really want to have to experience what it was like to be a girl who failed every class and then had to repeat a grade. You understand.

I'd also made a commitment to offer advice only from the Bible, even if I couldn't directly say that's where I found my answers. Because if you're a Christian, you know that's where all the good stuff comes from. As I shuffled through the papers, I laughed at some of the questions, felt sad about others, and prayed for the people who'd sent them in. Which should I choose? All of a sudden, the perfect—I mean perfect—question popped out at me. The best part was I didn't even have to learn this lesson! I was 100 percent dead certain God wouldn't make me. Why not? Because I'd already learned it!

Now for the answer from the Bible. I thumbed through the back of mine, in the concordance, but I couldn't find what I wanted. So I popped open my laptop with the screen saver of the newspaper staff—focused, of course, on Jack. After logging on to wireless, I clicked on a favorite: my Bible search program.

After a few minutes, I found exactly the verse I wanted: 1 Samuel 16:7. "The Lord doesn't see things the way you see them. People judge by outward appearance, but the Lord looks at the heart." I typed up my answer and e-mailed it to Jack.

I hoped the Aristocats would read that column.

# Chapter 4

Asking for Trouble column, Thursday, January 7:

**D**ear **Asking for Trouble,** For the longest time I've wanted a part-time job. I kept looking around for the right opportunity, and after some months, I finally got a call back. The job would be working part-time after school as secretarial help for a small insurance company. The pay is great for someone my age. But I don't know about my future boss. She's kind of frumpy looking, a bit old-fashioned. Her clothes are definitely old-school, and the computers and phones in the office are absolutely ancient. I want to be a real up-and-coming professional, and I'm afraid I might not get the training I'd like here. Should I take the job or keep looking?

Sincerely,
*Underemployed?*

♡

**D**ear **Employed,** Congratulations on your new job! You should feel good about landing a job after many months of hoping and looking. I do understand your disappointment. You thought it would be a certain way . . .. and it's not. Totally understandable. But consider this: what if the fact that she's not overspending on some things means she can hire you to help out in the office? This not only gives you good training, it also allows her to get more work done and make more money. Sounds like someone to learn from, right? Give it a chance, and don't judge the office and its equipment too quickly. Things aren't always on the inside what they seem on the outside.

# Chapter 5

After I finished picking up the leftover newspapers on Thursday afternoon, I decided to head to Fishcoteque for a well-deserved break and a little refreshment. I wished I had someone to go with me. But I didn't.

I folded up my Au Revoir bag and slipped it into my book bag. It was starting to wear thin from holding all the papers every Thursday and getting carted around in the rain. I wasn't sure how much longer it would hold up. But I knew for a fact I couldn't go back to using that smelly old yellowed bag the newspaper staff had originally wanted me to deliver the papers in.

On the way to the shop I saw a group of Aristocats walking together—or should I say a *herd* of them. Penny was with them too. It seemed that she was just slightly on the outside of the pack but definitely laughing along with them. It turned out that she was not only in my PE class with the rest of her clique but in my new history class too. But in that class, none of the others were with her. I'd been trying to work up the nerve to sit by her—since my other friendship options seemed limited. While she'd been nice, she'd also remained kind of distant. For starters, she hadn't returned my text last term, so that made me a little wary of pushing any kind of friendship on her.

The Aristocats turned the corner to the right, and I went left, then opened the door to the fish-and-chips shop. I was warmly embraced by the crispy scent and the smile of Jeannie, who was behind the counter.

"Well, look who it is," she said. "What'll it be then, luv? The usual?"

I nodded. "Fish-and-chips and a Fanta." I extracted three British pounds and ten pence—or ten p, as they say—from my book bag and paid her. Then I sat down at an empty booth.

After texting my mom to let her know where I was and when I'd be home, I looked around me. Most of the other booths were filled with teenagers—friends and couples mainly—because it was still the middle of the workday. There were live DJs on the weekends, but during the week a high-quality stereo pumped out British pop from the back area, which was usually filled with guys playing darts, most of whom seemed, oddly, to have extra-long bangs. I reached over and opened the neatly folded, used newspaper that someone had left on the table for the next person to read. I loved that about Wexburg, as opposed to London. People were very considerate.

I read the Auntie Agatha column—naturally—and hoped that the Aristocats had read *my* advice column and seen themselves in it. Hopefully they'd learn not to judge people by their looks instead of their insides. For example, certain persons who'd had a very bad hair day when they'd returned to school after Christmas holidays.

Then I turned the page to my second-favorite section, Living, which included the fashion page. Most of the time the fashion news was reprinted from the *Times* of London, and today was no different. However, there was one local column way down in the right-hand corner of the page.

Jeannie brought my fish-and-chips and Fanta.

"Thank you," I said.

"Anything for you, luv." As she bustled away, I folded the paper back and read the article more closely.

**London News**

# Designer Peter Chen

Up-and-coming London designer Peter Chen plans to shoot a fashion layout at The Beeches, the local family seat of Lord and Lady Gorm Strauss. The shoot done at the estate will feature clothing from his new line and is one of several photo sessions around the country in advance of London Fashion Week. As industry insiders know, London Fashion Week features couture designs from British and international designers and is held at various parks, museums, and other venues throughout London.

That was it. A tiny little article in the corner of the fourth page of the third section of the paper. To someone else, it probably meant nothing. They might have ignored it completely or even used it to wipe away fish-and-chips grease.

But not me. I was a longtime subscriber to *Teen Vogue*, a fashion window-shopper extraordinaire, a girl who spent all her hard-earned babysitting money on recent designs. I was also a girl desperate to have her own byline in the school paper—not just an anonymous advice column but something I could take credit for. Maybe then I would have more in common with someone like Penny. And I had to admit, not that I was proud of the fact, that it would be nice to scoop Hazelle too, since she had been nothing but sour milk to me. I knew that no one—not even my very fashionable mentor, Melissa—covered fashion for the school paper.

My assignment was clear. I had to find a way into that photo shoot. And then get Jack to allow me to write a feature article for the Wexburg Academy *Times*.

# Chapter 6

By the next Monday, the second week back after Christmas holidays, my new schedule felt a little more settled. Sure, there were a few, uh, wrenches in the whole thing. A very embarrassing one that I hadn't anticipated. And one great one, which I hadn't figured on either.

First period. Maths, of course. I didn't chew gum in there anymore, but I did slip the occasional stick to Brian now and again. He promised he wouldn't chew it till the end of the period. So when I saw him chomping away in class, I could only hope it was a spit wad or an eraser; otherwise I was going to have to cut him off.

"Savvy," he said. "Have you ever noticed how Mr. Thompson is always rubbing his head?"

I looked. It was true. He did often rub the top of his head. "Stress? Dandruff?" I guessed aloud.

"Or maybe . . . his horns are emerging!" Brian joked.

I shook my head at him. Guys were guys. As for girls, well, Hazelle would barely look at me in class. I wished she'd talk to me. I could give her some tips on avoiding that bloodred lipstick she wore.

Second period, PE. Every day when I walked in, the Aristocats were already lined up along the mirrored counter, monopolizing every single outlet for their hair appliances and leaving the rest of us to use the length mirrors at the end of the lockers with no outlet at all. Gwennie didn't need one—her cornrows always stayed perfect. Jill had the long, naturally straight hair the rest of us craved. I gazed longingly at the Aristocats' hot straighteners and pulled my hair back into a ponytail. Thankfully it fell into just the right place. Gwennie gave me the thumbs-up.

Third period, science: archaeology unit. Unfortunately, I accidentally dropped several of the precisely shaped rocks for the model meant to represent Stonehenge. No one thought it was funny when I suggested that Stonehenge, a point of national pride, might actually look better with a few more, but smaller, rocks. I spent the rest of the period with the superglue.

At lunch I sat next to Melissa at the newspaper table. As a year twelve, she didn't have to wear a uniform every day anymore like those of us who were a year or more younger. She always looked stylish and smelled faintly like the grapefruit shampoo she'd told me she used. "Hey, Savvy, how was your holiday?"

"Really nice," I said.

"Was Father Christmas good to you?" she teased. She'd had me help her with an article about Father Christmas the month before—in fact, he and I had formed an understanding of sorts.

"He was," I said, smiling.

"I'll keep my eyes open for another piece for us to work on together," she said.

I said nothing—yet. But if things worked out my way, I had just the idea in mind.

After lunch, fourth period was composition and literature. I loved our teacher, Mrs. Beasley. "Here you are, Miss Smith," she said, handing back one of my papers. She'd neatly written *Fine work* across the top. I'd never told anyone—not even Jen—how much I feared having a teacher, or anyone else, say my writing was bad. Because if it was true, what would happen to my dream?

Fifth period, French. Disaster. Everyone in England had already taken several years of language, so I was behind. That meant the other students in my class were two years younger than I was. I had to walk down the hall that connected the upper school with the lower school. The kids were short. They all stared at me. Enough said.

And then . . . sixth period. History, which I loved. When I walked in on Monday, I saw Penny, head down over her desk, sketching something on a notepad. I took a deep breath and sat next to her.

"Hi, Penny."

She looked up, her smile genuine. "Hullo, Savvy."

That's all she said. *Well, come on, Penny. Do I have to do all the work?*

"What are you drawing?" I asked.

She pulled herself away from her notebook so I could see her sketches.

"Wow, that's great," I said. "Are those your own designs?" There were several models on the page, the first one with a pair of plain flared pants, the second with a tailored shirt added, the third with a big hobo bag over her shoulder.

She nodded. "They are."

I stared at the sketches. "How about adding a long, chunky necklace?"

She studied me for a minute, startled, I think. "I think that's great," she said. She drew it in. "So you like fashion, then?"

It dawned on me that except for Fridays, when we could wear what we wanted, she'd never seen me in anything except my uniform. So she couldn't really know me. "I love fashion," I said. "I'd give anything to go to the Peter Chen show at the end of next month. It's coming here, you know."

She nodded. "I know. It's at Ashley's estate."

"Your *friend* Ashley?" I dropped my voice as Miss Nodding came into the room. Class would start soon.

"Yes, at my friend Ashley's estate. The Beeches."

Ah. Ashley was an Aristocat. My heart—and my hopes—fell. "Nice place?" I asked.

"Beautiful," she said. "You can see it for yourself if you like."

"What do you mean?" I asked, praying that

Miss Nodding would continue to do her filing or pick her teeth or twiddle her papers or do whatever else she was doing besides starting class.

"They have to hold an open house once a month. The Beeches is on the National Trust. Tax deduction, you know."

I nodded as if I deeply understood tax deductions for British estates. "Ah, yes," I said, in what I hoped was a knowing tone of voice.

"The open house is this Thursday evening. Anyone can attend. Would you like me to come with you?"

And just like that, I was on the road to a friend. I hoped. And on the way to The Beeches for the first—but hopefully not the last—time.

"I'd love to." I sat back and started to take notes as Miss Nodding began to talk about Henry VIII.

I was going to The Beeches. In three days. With Penny. It was all unbelievable, really—everything was going just fine. Perfectly. Without a hitch.

# Chapter 7

Thursday after school I picked up all the news-papers from the distribution stands. School rule—they didn't want copies of the Wexburg Academy *Times* flying all over the grounds after the school day was done.

"Hardly any papers left," I told Jack as I triumphantly returned to the newspaper staff room.

"Let's have a look." He peered into my quickly-becoming-shabby Au Revoir delivery bag. "Not bad!" he agreed.

Hazelle sat nearby, pretending to concentrate on her research, but I could see her ears twitching as she eavesdropped on Jack and me. She was sucking on a menthol cough drop. Its medicinal, minty scent was so strong it cleared my nose from across the room. Even if her ears were twitching, I had to ask him. I had no choice, no matter who was listening. Because tonight was the night I was going to The Beeches.

I swallowed my gum so it wouldn't get in the way and jumped right in. "I was wondering. There's a large fashion shoot being held at the end of next month at The Beeches. A new London designer, Peter Chen, is coming. It would be big news as part of London Fashion Week."

"Yes . . . ," he responded.

"We've been trying to reach more readers. Well, I think a lot of girls would be interested in that story. I'm going to The Beeches tonight. If I were able to get a couple of tickets to the fashion show at the end of next month, would you let me cover it for the paper?"

"Possibly, Savvy. Possibly."

At that, Hazelle began to cough. I looked at her to make sure she hadn't swallowed the cough drop down the wrong tube. She seemed to recover quickly, though.

"Get the tickets first," he said. "Then we'll talk." He sent *that smile* in my direction, and I sent a warm one back.

As I slipped into my jacket before leaving,

Hazelle turned toward me. "You shouldn't make it seem like you're anything special because you're going to Ashley's. It's not like she invited you. It's an open house. Anyone can go."

I nodded. "Anyone could go, Hazelle. You could too, if you wanted to."

"I have no interest in going to her house or to that fashion shoot," she said before turning back to her keyboard.

I smiled. I was a reformed little-white-lie teller. So I recognized an unreformed one immediately.

# Chapter 8

"Can I come too?" Louanne pleaded as I got dressed. My bedroom was littered with discarded outfits. A few potential candidates still lay across my bed. I needed the outfit to look perfect and perfectly my style. But what exactly *was* my style? I suddenly felt very unsure.

"Sorry, kiddo, you can't come," I said.

"But I like the beach," she insisted. Growl ran through a haystack of clean clothes on the floor, tossing them on himself and then rolling on his back.

I glared at him but then laughed at Louanne. "It's not the beach. You know how people name their houses and stuff here? Like our house is Kew Cottage? Ashley's house is called The

35

Beeches, like beech trees, silly. Not sand and ocean."

"Oh. Well. That's not as fun. But still, Savvy. Mom and Dad are so busy now, it's boring if you're not here. Dad's working on that project on the computer, and Mom's working on her library fund-raiser."

"Play with Growl . . . I mean Giggle."

"I can't even take him for a walk alone," she said mournfully.

"Sorry, kid." I looked at my clock. "I'll tell ya what. Tomorrow after school I'll go with you so you can take him for a nice long walk, okay?"

She nodded, taking whatever concession she could. I hung one of my old necklaces around her neck, and she smiled when I said she could keep it. Then I finally settled on a pencil skirt with a peasant blouse and bangle bracelets. I stood in front of the mirror. Looked good. Looked like me. But was I up-to-date enough?

"Mom!" I ran down the hall. "Can I borrow a purse?"

She nodded and waved at me, then turned back to her cell phone, or *mo-bile*, as the Brits called them. I went into her closet and found a hobo bag that I thought would work. I peeked inside. It was empty, so I took it back to my room and stashed my phone and wallet and lip gloss in it.

"Ready?" Dad dangled the car keys in front of me.

"Ready," I said.

# Chapter 9

We drove the short distance to the Gorm Strauss estate. We approached a long drive of beige crushed gravel. The driveway was guarded on either side by tall, thin beech tree "soldiers."

"I feel like we've been driving down this driveway for a long time," Dad said after a minute.

"Yeah. It's bigger than our whole street, that's for sure," I answered. Suddenly I wasn't sure if this was a great idea. What if something happened and Penny didn't show up?

We arrived at the far side of the circular driveway, and there were about a dozen cars parked out front already, including one cute sports car my dad couldn't take his eyes off of. The building was huge, square, made of buttery stone. I know that according to England's standards it wasn't right to call it a castle, but where I come from— Seattle—we'd definitely call this a castle.

Dad pulled up to a long stone staircase in front. The house was ablaze with lights shining out of every window, and I could hear classical music drifting through the open door. "Sure you want to go in? Want me to come in with you?" he asked.

"I'm fine," I said. "Penny promised to arrive ten minutes before I did so I wouldn't be there by myself."

I knew he would have come in with me if I'd wanted him to, but he looked relieved. He'd been busily working on his new project when we left. "Call me when you're ready to come back," he said.

"I will." I grabbed Mom's hobo bag and stepped out of the car, counting four sets of twelve steps, with three landings, before I reached the top. A uniformed man greeted me.

"Welcome to The Beeches, miss," he said. "The open rooms are all on the lower floor, as indicated by the notices." He extended his arm to point to one of the neatly calligraphed signs.

"Thank you," I said. Was I supposed to curtsy

or something? Good grief. I walked into the entry room, where a few other people were looking at the artwork on the walls. I scanned the room. No Penny.

There were several long hallways extending off the entry hall; I picked one and followed a sign to an open room. There was a roaring fire in a huge fireplace, along with several signs indicating important works of art. Parts of the room were cordoned off like in a museum. A young couple stood nearby. I decided to see if they could help me find the others my age.

"Is there a main room where everyone begins the tour?" I asked politely.

The man turned toward me and smiled coldly. "I couldn't say, I'm sure." He then took the elbow of the woman next to him—who reminded me of a thin Thoroughbred horse—and steered her down the hallway, leaving me alone in the room.

I heard some younger voices down the next hall, so I headed there. A perfectly groomed girl was standing in the room next to a tea trolley. She looked . . . familiar. I stared for a minute.

"Can I help you?" she asked. Then she stared back at me. "Do I know you?"

Suddenly I realized who she was. "You're in

my French class," I said. Which made her two or three years younger than I was.

She nodded. "Oh, yes. You're the American. My sister was talking about you. Come along with me." She headed down the hallway, and I followed like an obedient pet.

# Chapter 10

The girl led me into a large living area, where there were four girls sitting on a pink satin couch.

As soon as Penny saw me, she jumped up, but she was the only one who stood. "Savvy! When did you get here?"

"Just now," I said. I wasn't going to tell them that I'd been wandering in circles like the Israelites in the desert.

"Let me introduce you," Penny said. "This is Chloe—" she pointed to a thin redhead—"and Kylie. And of course Ashley, who lives here."

Ashley sat in a large armchair alone, not on the pink couch with the others. Like a throne, it occurred to me. A silver tray with unused teacups on it perched on a stand next to her. "Care for something to drink?" she asked.

I looked around. No one else was drinking tea. "No thanks," I said. It must have been the right answer, because she smiled.

First test passed.

"Savvy wants to write an article for the Wexburg Academy *Times* on the Peter Chen fashion shoot coming here next month," Penny said.

*Thank You for sending Penny ahead of me, Lord.*

"Has the paper's editorial staff agreed to cover the fashion shoot . . . and the house and my family?" Ashley inquired.

Just for a minute I was tempted to tell the world's tiniest little lie, but I knew that would make for big trouble. "There are a number of people who are very excited about the possibility," I answered as honestly as I could. The number being exactly two: me and Hazelle, even though she wouldn't admit it. Because whether she liked fashion or not, it was a big story, and she knew it.

Ashley nodded. "I'll show you around if you'd like to have a look." When she stood, I noticed that the fabric of the chair she'd been sitting in was exactly the same as the draperies and wallpaper behind it, and in fact, the chair almost disappeared into the background.

I tried not to be nervous as I followed her. I hoped my new Tahitian vanilla deodorant was as effective as it promised to be.

"Much of the fashion shoot will be done on the grounds," she said, swinging her curtain of black hair behind her as she walked. Her hair was long and straight. It never had a clip or a bow or a highlight or anything in it. It was shiny, though. I'd give her that.

"This suite of rooms will be used as well." She opened a door that didn't have an Open sign on it, so I figured it was a private part of the house. A butler was clearing dishes from a sleek, dark table that could have seated everyone I'd met in the past year.

Just then two little Pomeranians scurried up, barely a foot off the floor. One of them looked at me and bared her teeth. The other one started growling and doing a low crawl in my direction.

*Oh no. Not dogs.* Ashley looked at me, and I had the feeling that this was test number two.

"Are these your dogs?" I asked.

"Yes," she said. "I adore dogs. Do you have any?"

*Thank you, Louanne.* "We have a dog named Giggle at home. He was one of the first things we added to our family when we moved here."

She led me back to the pink room, where Penny and the others were talking. When we entered the room, all talk stopped, and the air hung uncomfortably in the room. I got the distinct impression it hadn't been Ashley they'd been discussing.

Penny stood up. "Savvy, I'm just about to go. Would you like a ride home?"

I nodded, thankful. "Let me just text my parents and make sure."

"Fine," she said. "I'll go get Mum. She's chatting with Lady Gorm Strauss."

"Thanks again, Ashley."

"Think nothing of it," she said, but I knew that's not what she meant. She still held the cards, er, the tickets to the photo shoot. She hadn't said anything at all about getting me in.

As I left, I heard one of the other girls sniff the air right behind me and then ask, "Do you have vanilla candles burning? All of a sudden I smell something vanilla."

I quickly slipped my arms into my coat sleeves and held my arms close to my side as I waited by the front door for Penny and her mum, who then drove me home in that cute little sports car.

"Do you think she'll get me the tickets?" I asked Penny in a low voice as we sat in the backseat.

She shrugged. "I dunno, Savvy. You'll know tomorrow. Ashley doesn't waste time."

# Chapter 11

The next day, Friday, after science, I took my lunch sack and headed toward the newspaper staff table, where I usually sat. But Penny reached out her hand and grabbed my arm. "Savvy, sit with us today," she said.

I looked at the Aristocats' table. With *them*? Did everyone agree? Chloe smiled at me briefly before turning back to a head-to-head discussion with one of the others. It was funny—I noticed from that vantage point that all their heads appeared the same. Smooth, long hair of varying colors, tucked behind ears or hanging straight down. I glanced at Penny, who smiled encouragingly, and then I sat next to her.

"That's it, then," she said. "Ready for old Henry VIII in history today?"

I smiled and began to take my lunch out of my bag. "Yes. I love history. I can't wait to get to the part where he starts lopping off his wives' heads."

The table went quiet, watching me unpacking my lunch. I noticed that most of them had very little lunch or none at all. Compared to them, I felt like I'd packed a hearty farmer's lunch with my sandwich, apple, cookie, and bottled water. I neatly slid everything except the bottle of water into my bag. As soon as I did, everyone went back to chatting. I willed my stomach not to growl and hoped that I had stuck an extra pack of gum in my book bag to make it till I got to Fishcoteque.

Just then Hazelle walked by, and in spite of my silent and fervent prayers, she stopped right in front of me. "Why are you sitting there, Savvy?" she asked.

I shrugged and said nothing, not really sure what the answer was. She gave me a smug, "I know what you're doing" look and moved on.

"Since you love history, I can see why you're friends with her," one of the snottier Aristocats said to me. I hadn't even been aware that she'd heard my comment earlier.

"Why?" I asked. I didn't bother to tell her that Hazelle and I were not friends. Not that I hadn't tried to befriend Hazelle. But maybe it was time to move on to greener fields anyway. *A good analogy,* I thought, looking longingly in the direction of my sandwich, *for someone with a farmer's lunch.*

"Hazelle's father is a security guard at the British Museum in London," Penny said. She didn't seem to be siding with me, but she wasn't really siding with them, either.

"That must be where she gets her clothes from! Antiques from discarded exhibits!" one of the other girls said. At that, nearly the whole table laughed. Not me, though, and not Penny, who still stared straight ahead.

"Savvy," Ashley Gorm Strauss started, "I spoke with Mother last night and asked her if it might be a good idea to have the Chen fashion shoot featured in the Wexburg Academy *Times.* I explained to her that The Beeches and our family would be positively portrayed—" she paused and looked at me meaningfully before continuing—"in addition to the coverage of the designs, of course. I'll get two tickets to you next week." Then she turned back to one of her other friends and began talking. Just like that, my royal interview was over.

But who cared? I got the tickets. I'd get the scoop. I'd write the article with my *own* byline— my own name—and I'd be a real journalist at last. I'd waited for this for years.

Penny glanced at me out of the corner of her eye and grinned, and I grinned back.

A minute later Ashley stood up and headed toward the door with a gaggle of the other Aristocats. Everyone began to stand up at the same time, having been given the signal from the top.

Ashley looked over at me. "Just a little helpful tip," she said. "Everyone there will be completely decked out. You'll want to be stylish too, I know." She faced me straight on, so I didn't know if she was saying I wasn't stylish already or what.

"You won't want to bring anyone else who's not prepared to fit in fashionably either," she said, fixing her gaze on Hazelle.

I got the message all right.

# Chapter 12

We'd only been going to our new church since
Christmas, but I liked the preacher and I loved
the music. It was funny to hear him say, "Eye-
sigh-ah" instead of "Eye-zay-uh" for Isaiah, and
it just seemed too cool to hear preaching with
a British accent. This week, since everyone was
pretty much back from Christmas holidays, we'd
decided to go to the Sunday school classes after
the service.

"You know where you're going?" Mom asked.

I nodded. She was dropping Louanne off at
her class, and then she and Dad were going to an
adult theology class. I knew the high school class
was right off of the center area with the huge
fireplaces and comfy couches. I certainly didn't

want my parents escorting me there. Although, truth be told, I would rather have waited in the car for the next hour than walk in.

But I did walk in. The room was cool enough. There were wide-screens on the wall and couches and a coffee and tea bar—even though it seemed to be shut—and lots of chairs, which rapidly filled up. Because the church was nearly in London, there was a wider variety in the backgrounds of the people— Asian and Indian, which I was used to, being from Seattle, and some from island nations and African backgrounds too. In a way, it made me feel more welcome. I wasn't the one "different" person here, "the American." We were all Christians; some had always lived in England and some were from other places, but now we were all here together.

Sitting by myself in the second-to-last row, however, I didn't feel very together with anyone. As the rows began to fill in on either side of me with people who obviously already knew each other, I didn't feel crowded. I felt alone. But the youth pastor mentioned something about the music and coffeehouse night the high schoolers held on Wednesday nights. That sounded cool. And maybe I'd make a friend if I could go then, when it wasn't so crowded.

Afterward my family met in the lobby and walked to the car.

"I knew someone from school in my class!" Louanne said. "I was really surprised to see her, and we sat together the whole time. She knows a lot of people. She's going to introduce me."

"Good!" Mom said. "I found out that there is a ladies' Bible study. I'm hoping to ask Vivienne to come sometime. And your father—" she elbowed him—"was invited to be on the greeting committee."

"Not," Dad said. He kept his eyes on the road, but I saw a little smile. "How about you, Savvy?"

I pictured going on Wednesday. I'd bring my guitar, of course, and there'd be a spot for me right away on the worship team. Their guitar player would have just quit. Or . . . maybe he'd hear me practicing and decide to let me do the lead for a while. I'd start hanging out with the rest of the band, and we'd compose together.

"Savvy!" Dad called out. "Did you hear me? I asked how your class was."

"Oh. Okay. . . . But they meet on Wednesday nights for coffee, worship, and discussion. Can I go?"

"We'll see. Someday we'll try it," Mom said

breezily. "One step at a time. It's a long drive. And things are really busy right now."

I knew what "We'll see" meant. It meant after we took our six-month around-the-world cruise and appeared on a trivia game show and handily won every category against the Oxford graduates, *then* we could go on Wednesday nights. In other words, not anytime soon.

Meanwhile, I'd keep slouching in the back row.

Mom's mo-bile rang and she answered. "Oh yes, Maude. Yes, we'll be home in about thirty minutes. Let yourself in, of course." Then she hung up. "I hope I tidied the house well enough," she muttered. "I thought she was coming a bit later."

"Aunt Maude is coming today?" I groaned. "Why?"

Louanne looked at me too sweetly. She knew.

# Chapter 13

"Hello, dears. I've just got lunch ready for us, then." Aunt Maude bustled around the house wearing my mother's apron, which seemed to put my mother off a bit. Maude wasn't really our aunt—she was a good friend of our grandma's—and she rented this house to us while we were living in London. She'd moved farther out into the country and traveled with a bunch of her widowed friends.

"Oh, lunch . . . good," Dad said, oblivious to my mom's obvious discomfort that someone had been rummaging around in her pantry and fridge. "What are we having?"

"I've just come from Scotland," Aunt Maude said, "so I thought haggis would be nice. I've brought some with me."

The last thing I'd eaten from Scotland had been butter cookies that came in a pretty red tin. So I was prepared to like haggis.

"What's haggis?" Louanne asked.

"Sheep innards," Aunt Maude said cheerfully as she heaped a steaming plate of guts onto our table. I felt ready to keel over, and my mother looked as if all her blood had rushed down to her toes. "Don't worry, dears. I've washed them well," she said.

"I'm a vegetarian, remember," Louanne squeaked out.

"Yes, I've got a lovely fruit salad for you and some Scottish butter cookies."

Drat that Louanne and her vegetarianism.

"I've also got bacon roly-poly," Aunt Maude said as we sat down.

Okay, now we were talking. I love bacon.

Dad prayed and we dug in. Maude sliced me some of the roly-poly. It was good and moist. "Does it have mayo on it too?" I asked, thinking that this was a cool way to make a spiral BLT.

"Oh no. Suet." Maude sliced herself a thick serving.

"Suet? Isn't that something you feed to birds?"

"The fat around the sheep's kidneys," she informed us matter-of-factly.

I stopped a swallow halfway down my throat, but I knew I'd be grounded if I spit it out. I cut the rest of the roly-poly into little bits and covered them with a large serving of salad. Then I looked longingly at Louanne's fruit. She pulled her plate out of my reach but did hand over a slice of mango.

During the course of lunch, I found out why Aunt Maude was here—besides off-loading sheep guts on us. She was taking Louanne to her first practice dog show. She'd been a dog owner her whole life and had offered when she found out Louanne wanted to take Giggle. I had to admit that was kind of sweet, and I was glad for Louanne.

After they left, I went upstairs. A stack of the Wexburg Academy *Times* rested on my dresser, and I pulled out the last Asking for Trouble column and read it. I'd meant what I said about judging people from the inside. Not that Ashley had seemed to read it, based on her comment about Hazelle. But there wasn't anything wrong with making the most of your outside appearance too, right?

For example, I wanted to show up at the photo shoot looking my absolute best. In fact . . . this was a good time to change my style altogether!

Maybe there was a silver lining to hardly knowing anyone yet. *This* was my chance to reinvent myself. A new town—a new country! I could be whoever I wanted to be.

I looked in the mirror. First, I'd cut my long blonde hair. No! I'd highlight it. Platinum. I grinned widely. Thankfully I'd had my braces taken off before we left the States. But how to make them whiter? Laser whitening system—there was sure to be one in London. Or at the very least, high-quality whitening strips.

# Chapter 14

I felt the excitement rise in me like a fever. I reached under my bed, flopping my hand around till I'd located my well-thumbed fashion magazines. I needed to find my totally unique style. Now.

I got a pad of sticky papers out of my drawer and firmly pressed them onto styles I deemed potential winners. Then I noted them on a piece of art paper.

- Sporty librarian
- 50s starlet
- Punk preppy
- Classic rock
- Yacht club
- Poor Girl
- Rich Bohemian

my style

The only question was which one to start with. And how could I pull off these looks without spending too much of the money I'd been saving?

The only answer was a trip to London—the stores and the outdoor markets. Portobello Road. Miss Selfridge. Topshop. I could try out the runner-up outfits each Friday, the one day a week we didn't have to wear uniforms. And I'd wear the winning outfit to the shoot but not to school. It'd be a total surprise.

I gazed at my list and lost focus. Ashley wouldn't even recognize me. At first when I arrived at The Beeches, they'd think I was part of Peter Chen's crew. Ashley would ask me if she could help out in any way, and then I'd see the look of shock on her face when she realized it was . . . *moi*! Suddenly she'd realize how she'd underestimated me all along.

"Savvy!" Mom opened the door and shouted me out of my reverie. "I've been knocking on the door for a full minute. Are you all right?"

"Oh yeah, I'm fine."

"I'm going next door to Vivienne's to design the flyers. Dad's downstairs working. Let me know if you need anything, okay?"

I nodded and she shut the door. Maybe I

should go vegan, too. Yeah. Vegan. That would be different, unusual . . . It would set me apart. By the time Mom got home from Vivienne's, I'd have the shopping trip nailed down for her. She, of course, would say yes.

# Chapter 15

"No," Mom said. "I'm sorry, Savvy; there just isn't time this week."

"You're *alwaaays* too busy," I pleaded. I saw a flicker of guilt cross her eyes.

"I am busy lately," she admitted. "But, Savvy, you have to give me more than a few minutes', or days', notice when you want to do something. We can plan a trip to London next month. For sure."

"Next month? I can't wait that long. I need to buy some stuff—with my own money—and start gearing up. I'm making friends now. I want to wear these things on casual Fridays. And I need to show up looking good for that photo shoot. It's my first article—remember?"

"I remember," Mom said. "We will go before the photo shoot. Sometime."

"And in the meantime?"

"In the meantime, you can shop in the village."

The village. I was unlikely to find anything— even fake Coco Chanel or Ralph Lauren—in the village. Or a vegan cookbook. Maybe Ashley would ask her driver to take me to London.

Ha.

"I saw an ad for a botox clinic in London," I said. "The same place they do laser teeth whitening. You could get a little injection for that wrinkle between your eyes while my teeth get bright."

As soon as the words were half out of my mouth, I knew I'd made a fatal mistake. My mom's hand rushed to her forehead and started smoothing the wrinkle out. "Is it that bad? Really?"

I tried to protest that it wasn't bad at all and that I just thought an ounce of prevention was worth a pound of cure, but she was already rushing toward the mirror in the downstairs bathroom to check it out.

Conversation over.

Maybe Aunt Maude would come to the rescue. I shined a couple of leaves on her plants so they'd be looking spiffy when she came back. I propped up a few droopy branches. I even dusted. I wanted her in a good mood.

A few minutes later Aunt Maude and Louanne came bounding into the house, followed by an exhausted Growl, who immediately flopped on a sunny patch of the living room floor.

"Put him through the paces, huh?" I asked.

Louanne grinned. Her face was red from the winter air, but she looked happier than I'd seen her in a long time.

"He did great," she said. "He has one more practice on January 30, and then his first real dog show is next month. Will you help me walk him after school, Savvy? I can't go out of the block on my own."

Oh, man. I had my secret column to write and homework to do, which was a bear. Also this new clothing thing and trying to juggle the Aristocats and see if Penny and I could do some stuff together. "We'll see," I said. "It's a pretty busy time."

Her smile dampened just a little. Then she turned to hang her coat in the closet.

I turned to Aunt Maude. "Going into London anytime soon?" I asked hopefully.

"Oh no, dear. I hate traveling to London unless

absolutely necessary. The traffic is horrible. There are young thugs running around. And last time I was there, someone was spitting right on the pavement. No. It's the country for me."

I sighed. There went my next-to-last idea. I had only one more idea left, but I thought it was brilliant. I'd wait till my parents had settled down for the night and eaten a good—non-Scottish—dinner. And then I'd float my plan.

# Chapter 16

My parents were sitting in the kitchen, winding down for the night and up for the week. Dad was putting a new bottle of tomato juice in the fridge, and Mom was scribbling a grocery list.

"So, I had a superbrilliant idea. You guys are busy, and so am I. We both have things we need to get done. So it makes sense to divide and conquer, right?"

Dad looked at me with a wary expression. "What do you mean?"

"Well, I need some things in London. So I was thinking . . . how about I just take the Underground in by myself? Do a little tooling around in the markets, some of the stores. Make my purchases and—" I snapped my fingers—"like that, I'll be home."

"No," both my parents said in eerie, unplanned unison.

"Why not?" I pleaded. "It's so easy."

"You heard Aunt Maude," Mom said. "There are thugs in London."

"Mom, please. There are thugs at school. There are thugs everywhere. But I'd be going in broad daylight, and London is the safest city in the world. You said so yourself when we first moved here."

Louanne walked into the room with a concerned look on her face. "People spit on the sidewalk. Aunt Maude said so."

Since when was Aunt Maude the source of all knowledge? "I'll wear boots," I said.

"No, Savvy," my dad said. "Not yet. Soon . . . but not yet. No subway on your own."

And with that, each of them filtered out of the room—Dad to the telly, Mom to her mo-bile, and Louanne to comb out Growl.

I flicked off the kitchen lights and prepared to leave the room myself. As I did, I saw an Underground schedule lying on the countertop. I looked at it for a minute and almost walked away. Then I stepped back, folded it in half, and put it in the back pocket of my jeans.

# Chapter 17

Monday was usually the day I spent writing my Asking for Trouble column, but since Jack had told me that I wouldn't be doing one this week— the paper was running a full edition on sports— I would have a little unexpected free time. In Seattle, Mondays had been a good day to hang out with my friends. I thought maybe I could try to work that out here, too.

At lunch I headed over to the newspaper staff table, but the guys were talking about sports. Melissa and Hazelle were sitting at other tables today. I stood there, a little disoriented for a minute, not sure what to do. Then Penny waved me over.

"Come sit with us," she said. I hadn't really seen much of the Aristocats since Ashley promised to give me the tickets. Note: she still hadn't done so, and I didn't think I could bug her about it. But maybe if I was sitting at the table, right in front of her, it would remind her.

"Thanks," I said. Since I was a newly converted vegan, my lunch looked a little lighter to their prying eyes. A bag of shredded lettuce. A paltry offering of Wheat Thins. Orange quarters. Ashley fixed her eyes on my lunch and then, with a nod of approval, went back to her conversation.

It felt slightly slimy, actually, to be getting her approval. It was an unsettling feeling, and it didn't bring the pleasure I'd thought it would.

"How was your weekend?" Penny asked.

"Very good," I told her. "Hung out at home and did some homework. Played the guitar. Went to church."

"Ohh . . . ," she said. I wasn't sure if the *ohh* was because I'd gone to church, hung out with my family, or hadn't mentioned any friends. I thought maybe the latter.

"One thing I've been spending a lot of time on is fashion," I said, nibbling like Peter Rabbit. "I came up with a lot of cool styles I'm going to try."

"Really? That sounds exciting. Tell me about

them." Penny ate a cookie—er, *biscuit. Weren't sweets forbidden by the Aristocats? Daring, Penny. Very daring.*

I gave her a list of some of the things I was looking for, and she seemed enthusiastic. "Hey, would you like to do some shopping with me today?" I asked. "It's only in the town square, but . . ."

"I'm sorry," she said. "Normally I'd love to, but I have a makeup lesson for piano today. Text me sometime and we'll hang out."

*Was this the time to bring it up?* "You know, I did text you once," I said, "but you didn't answer, so . . . I figured maybe, you know, you weren't cool with it."

She looked surprised. "Really? I don't remember getting a text from you. What number did you try?"

I whipped out my phone and showed her.

"Oh no," she said. "You've put sevens where there should be ones." She handed my phone back to me and pulled out her own. "I think I've got your number too. Let me text you and see."

Penny opened her phone and texted me.

Hullo Savvy. Talk soon.

"Better?"

"Better," I agreed. "We'll hang out another time."

We spent the rest of lunch chatting about friends and guys and fashion, and it flew by. At the end of the day, I was ready to conquer the vast metropolis of downtown Wexburg. I headed to the town square with a purpose.

The first store had . . . old ladies' clothes. I figured I found where Aunt Maude shopped when she's in town. And—with all due respect, because I really admire the old girl—I think the Queen probably bought some of those loopy hats here too.

Second store, smoke shop. Enough said. Pass.

The third store had some potential, but really everything was kind of bland. Your usual hoodies and T-shirts with supposed-to-be-funny sayings on them.

I finally made it to the post office, which was actually kind of like a drugstore. I waved to my friend Father Christmas—er, um, Tom, for the other eleven months of the year—and then searched for anything at all.

Okay, there were some cool reading glasses with thick, black rectangular rims. I put them on and squinted in the little mirror. I looked chic. Intelligent. So it wasn't exactly Ralph Lauren sporty librarian. But it was smart looking. I bought them and tucked them away till Friday.

# Chapter 18

Friday, lunchtime. Skinny brown khakis, crisp white shirt, small pearl earrings. I was making do with what I had. I slipped the glasses on—they were more powerful than I'd remembered—and tried to walk down the hallway to the Aristocats' lunch table. I nearly missed the door to the commons and tripped into a guy I barely knew.

"Oh, sorry," I said. I couldn't focus through the lenses. It felt like the time in school the year before when they'd made us wear "beer goggles" to simulate the sensation of being drunk. The idea was that we'd understand on a whole new level why we didn't want to do that.

I forced myself to concentrate and somehow made it to the table where Penny was, unless my sight was really messed up, already eating potato chips. Uh, that would be *crisps*, if you're British. I misjudged the distance to sit down and fell into her. My elbow landed on her bag of crisps, and the whole table turned to watch the fiasco as the crisps turned into potato confetti.

"First day with the new feet, Savvy?" Ashley asked, and everyone joined in laughing, as if on cue.

Needless to say, she did not hand over the tickets to the photo shoot.

After school I went home, took off the glasses, and slipped on my jeans. I needed comfort. And then, as promised, I took Louanne and Growl for a long training walk since my mother was next door at Vivienne's. When we were done, I texted Mom that I was going to Fishcoteque for a while to work on a short story I was writing.

"Can I come?" Louanne asked.

"Not this time," I answered. "Maybe another time."

I kept my coat and scarf on against the cold London rain and headed off down Cinnamon Street. The welcome greeting, even more than the steamy room, warmed my heart as I stepped inside.

"What'll it be, luv? The usual?"

My stomach was begging me to order fish. Or fried clams. Yum. Or those delectable little shrimp. But I was a vegan now. "No. Just mushy peas, some chips, and a Fanta, please."

She looked at me funny but wrote up the order. I reached into my back pocket to pull out a five-pound note and got something else instead.

The subway schedule.

I sat at an empty table and read the brochure, gently running my fingers down the creases and over the timetables. Next Saturday was January 30. My parents would be taking Louanne to her dog training event. It was half an hour into London and half an hour back, which left about three hours to shop, if I decided to do it.

Disobeying wasn't something I'd typically do. But this wasn't a typical situation. So maybe special circumstances applied.

# Chapter 19

Sunday mornings felt normal again. Even though my family had been scattered like pick-up sticks during the week, I felt whole and happy and close to them in church. The pastor was speaking on spiritual gifts. What was my spiritual gift? I'd always wondered. I doodled in my bulletin around the verse, 1 Corinthians 12:28, while he continued speaking.

Here are some of the parts God has appointed for the church:

first are apostles,

I wasn't even sure what an apostle was. I drew a line through it.

second are prophets,

I wished I knew the future. Maybe. Or . . . not. I drew a line through this one too.

third are teachers,

Maybe.

then those who do miracles,

No. Not unless you count setting Jen up with the cutest boy in junior high last year. They were still going out. So maybe that was a miracle. But not a spiritual gift. I drew a line through it.

those who have the gift of healing,

No.

those who can help others,

I steadied my pencil here for a long time before moving on.

those who have the gift of leadership,

I don't know. I'd have to look at this more closely.

those who speak in unknown languages.

Well, if my grade in French was any indication, I couldn't even do well with known languages. I put a line through it.

I did go back and circle "those who can help others." That's what my column was all about. Maybe I could use that gift for God in other ways too. *Thank You, Lord,* I prayed. *For using me at all.*

After the service I went to Sunday school and, having been nudged by the Spirit in the service, decided to be brave and introduce myself to someone. There was a girl wearing a gold and nutmeg silk shirt standing with one other person, laughing contagiously. When she sat down alone, I sat next to her.

"Is anyone sitting here?" I asked.

"No, go right ahead," she said. She had a tiny diamond nose stud that flashed against the creamy brown of her skin. "My name is Supriya."

"Savvy," I answered. "Have you been going here long?"

"Not too long," she said. "A couple of months. You?"

"Totally new," I admitted.

Then class started.

Afterward a couple of Supriya's friends came up to chat with her, but before she was drawn away, she said, "I hope I see you on Wednesday night. There's more time to talk then."

On the way home I brought up going on Wednesday nights again, but I didn't get a real yes or no. I wasn't going to let it spoil my church high, though. *I still want to help others for You, Jesus,* I prayed.

*I'm going to help you too,* I felt His presence say in my heart. *Very soon.*

# Chapter 20

When the Lord says soon, He means soon.

The next day I sat with Penny at lunch. We brought some history work to finish up together. It was so cool being in that class together, especially since she had the same kind of fascination with the wives of Henry VIII that I did. She taught me the British schoolgirl rhyme to remember what happened to his six wives: "Divorced, beheaded, died, divorced, beheaded, survived. Ol' Hal had a hard time keeping the girls."

Anyway, lunch was almost over when Hazelle walked by and reminded me that I needed to be at the newspaper office early the next morning. To help clean up. It wasn't a very nice thing to say, really, because I knew she was just trying to make the point in front of the Aristocats that I was the low girl on the team. But after she walked by, Ashley started in on her.

"What does *she* do on the paper? Cover agricultural livestock shows?" The table burst out in laughter. Hazelle hadn't been nice to me. But neither had these girls. I wasn't strong enough to say anything, and I wasn't sure what I could say anyway. But I was strong enough to get up and walk away.

I stood and ran my hands over my uniform—pleated navy blue skirt with contrasting green and maroon plaid. I rolled up my crisp white shirtsleeves and straightened the loose tie with the gold Wexburg Academy symbol embroidered on it. "I'd better get to class," I told Penny. "See you in history?"

Penny nodded but didn't stand to leave.

On the way to class I bumped into Jack. As always, standing close to him made my knees feel as rubbery as already-been-chewed gum.

"Hi, Savvy. I've missed seeing you round," he said. "Be at the staff meeting this afternoon?"

I nodded. *He'd missed me!*

"I've got a batch of questions for you. I'll e-mail them to you so you can go through them in private and see if there are new ones for the Asking for Trouble column."

"Okay," I said. "I'll have the copy to you by tomorrow night."

Jack started to leave, then paused. "Oh, Savvy." He turned around. "Are you planning to do that fashion shoot article or not? I've got to start thinking about layouts and content for next month."

"I'm going to do it," I said, hoping I sounded more confident than I felt. "I should have the tickets soon."

He held my gaze for a moment, the flash of doubt across his face eventually replaced by *that smile.* "Okay."

# Chapter 21

Ashley was in my next class, composition. She said nothing to me; I said nothing to her. We both kept our heads down and did our work as Mrs. Beasley droned on about sentence structure.

Ashley's younger sister was in my fifth period French class. She sat with the Aristokittens. I ignored her and concentrated on conjugating French verbs.

Last class of the day—my favorite, history. Penny was in there already, sitting in her usual seat, right across from my usual seat. I slid in.

She handed an envelope to me. "Here."

It was a heavy, ivory linen envelope with the calligraphed letters *GS* on it. "What's this?"

"Open it up."

I slid my pointer finger underneath the edge of the envelope and withdrew two tickets. "The Peter Chen show!"

Penny nodded. "Ashley gave them to me to give to you since you left lunch early."

"I had to," I said.

"I know," Penny said. "I get that. But I doubt Ashley even noticed why you did it. She figures it can't hurt to have her estate and family in the school paper. It might even boost her popularity. She wants it written up."

"Thanks, Penny. I couldn't have gotten these without you. Not only bringing them to me now, but introducing me to Ashley, inviting me to The Beeches—everything."

"It's nothing," Penny said. "We're friends. I wanted to help you finally write an article."

*We're friends. We're friends!* Those words were even better than the tickets, than my own byline on the article. Really. I had the greatest desire right then to share my secret with her—about the anonymous Asking for Trouble columns I'd been writing. But it wouldn't be right. "I'd like to pay you back somehow," I said. I noticed Miss Nodding come into the room, and she looked like she had a bee in her bonnet. We needed to wrap up our conversation fast.

"No need. But . . . Ashley did remind me that everyone there needs to be really fashion forward. To fit in with the shoot and also to make a good impression. As the guests of the Gorm Strausses."

"Oh, of course. I remember. I'll pay good attention to what I wear. Don't worry."

"And . . . whoever you bring with you." She looked at me meaningfully.

I knew what she was afraid of. On this point, at least, I could give her some relief. "I'm asking Melissa to help me. You know her? She's year twelve."

Penny literally sighed with relief. "Oh, oh yes. Good. Fantastic. She'll do. And, well, I hate to bring it up, but Ashley did feel certain that the article would feature The Beeches and her family in a positive way."

"I loved The Beeches," I said. "I'll talk about it in comparison to the high-quality fashion."

"Thank you, Savvy," she said quietly.

All of a sudden I became aware that it wasn't just me on the line—it was her, too. She'd been my ticket—in a way—into this event. I had no idea what her group of friends would do if things went poorly.

I'd make sure they didn't.

# Chapter 22

I screeched into the newsroom like a nervous hen after school, waving the envelope in my hand like I'd just won a million-dollar lottery, only I didn't gamble. Since the last bell had just rung, it was only Jack and Rodney and Hazelle and me in the room.

"Guess what these babies are?" I waved them at Jack. "Tickets to the fashion shoot, the Peter Chen fashion shoot! During London Fashion Week."

"Nice work, Savvy," Jack said. "We'll work on getting some adverts for the paper too. We should bring in some good money with that kind of high-profile piece. Maybe from some of the salons around here or some London shops, even."

"There are two tickets," I said. "I'd like to have

Melissa work with me on this since she was kind enough to ask me to help her with the Father Christmas piece last month. Is that all right?"

Suddenly, like Lazarus, Hazelle sprang from her dead position at her desk and said, "Hey. I'm supposed to have the next assignment. Right? Didn't you promise that to me, Jack?" Next thing I know she's standing right next to me, newly applied red lipstick overwhelming my field of vision.

*No, Lord. Not Hazelle. Remember? I already stood up for her once today.*

"I did say you could go next," Jack agreed with her. "But Melissa is more experienced."

"Yes, yes, more experienced," I heartily agreed, vigorously nodding my head.

"But she sent *you* to fact-gather last month, and *you're* not experienced at all," Hazelle pointed out.

"True," Jack said. "You and Hazelle could always go to the shoot and then Melissa could help you write it up and set type. Fair is fair. I did promise Hazelle. But . . . Savvy gets top billing on the article credits and byline."

Hazelle nodded her agreement.

No. This wasn't happening. What would Hazelle wear? Worse yet, what would I tell Penny, who I was sure had already told Ashley that I'd be bringing cool, superfashionable Melissa?

"It's settled, then. All right?"

No. It was not all right.

# Chapter 23

It was time to launch Operation HHH: Help Hazelle in a Hurry.

Tuesday. We all arrived early in the newspaper staff room. It was normally my job to tidy up around the place.

"Hi, Hazelle," I said as politely as possible. "I wondered if maybe you'd like to come over to my house next Monday and hang out. Talk about fashion things—" at this, Hazelle gave me a stink eye—"since we'll be doing a fashion article and all," I finished. I wanted to say, *"Come on over so I can give you a little background in an apparently foreign field."*

"Okay," she said reluctantly. "And I can teach you a thing or two about writing."

*Zing.*

I sweetly held out a bag full of hair products. "I had some extra products from my hair-care collection," I said. "Some of them are really good at, uh, smoothing down the frizzies." I willed myself not to look at her wiry brown hair.

Hazelle kept her hands at her side, refusing the bag. "Savvy, after your hairdo on the first day of this term, I think I'd better stick with my own regimen."

*Ouch.*

Wednesday. First period, maths. With Brian, my gum-chewing buddy, and Hazelle. I handed an extra piece of gum to Brian—for after class, of course—and sat next to Hazelle instead.

She seemed a little nervous, like I was a stalker or something, instead of someone initiating a friendship. So I went slowly. "Have you ever had your colors done?" I asked casually.

Her forehead wrinkled. "What?"

"You know. A color consultant compares your skin and hair colors with a big wheel and tells you what colors look best on you. I'm a summer. Or sometimes a winter."

"I'm a human, not a season," she said. "Don't forget to be in early tomorrow. We're printing extra papers, and you might need to take more than one trip to deliver them. By the way, your delivery bag seems to be falling apart."

I sighed. Yes, I knew. My expensive, once-favorite Au Revoir bag was giving its life for the newspaper. The way Operation HHH was going, I might be doing the same.

Thursday. I did get to the newspaper staff room early, and Melissa was already there making sure the folding machine ran smoothly. "Hey, Savvy. How's the week going? I hear you scored an amazing set of tickets for the Peter Chen fashion shoot. Way to go!"

I beamed. Her praise meant a lot to me. "I'm very excited. I wanted to bring you . . . ," I said softly. It was true, but there was no sense rubbing sand in Hazelle's eyes.

Melissa smiled. "I know. I'll help you with the write-up once you guys get the research done."

I nodded. I wished I could tell Melissa that I was the Asking for Trouble columnist—that in fact I'd already turned in a column for this week, and at this very moment, there were three questions sitting in my top dresser drawer waiting for me to answer. The buzz around the staff was that the column was the first one the girls at school read.

The guys read Rodney's sports column first, but then sometimes turned to the Asking for Trouble column in the weeks that it appeared, for counter-intelligence—that is, what girls were thinking.

But I had to keep it a secret. Which was why it was so vital that I got to write an article under my own name. It would only be fair.

Half an hour later Hazelle and I were stuffing the newspapers into my bag. I thought I'd try one more time. "So . . . are you more of a bracelet or necklace kind of girl?" I asked. Accessories would definitely help.

"I'm a book kind of a girl," she said snidely.

I looked her in the eye but spoke in a soft voice. "So am I, Hazelle. But I like fashion, too."

She looked at me with, I think, fresh eyes. "What kind of books do you read?"

"History is my favorite. Fiction. Romance."

She didn't say any more right then, just helped fill up the bag. I delivered the papers and came back for a refill. After we'd finished the second load, Hazelle said, "I'm still coming to your place on Monday, right?"

"Right." I'd have a game plan worked out by then.

Late that afternoon, after I'd collected the

papers from the distribution centers, I stopped in the newspaper room. Jack and Melissa were the only ones there, heads together over an article. The vibe was definitely . . . different.

"Hey, I wanted to let you know that there were hardly any papers left!" I said as I approached Jack's desk. "People are not only reading it more—they're taking it home."

"That's great, Savvy," Jack said. He flashed *that smile* at me, but I got the feeling I was interrupting something. "Maybe due to all the new columns?" He grinned, and I practically willed him to wink at me, because I knew he was talking about the secret advice column—*our* secret. Wink! Wink!

Alas, he didn't. He turned back to Melissa. After a minute, I slunk out and went home to do my homework, walk Giggle/Growl with Louanne, and pick out tomorrow's outfit.

After all, it was casual Friday. Time to debut a new look.

# Chapter 24

Today's outfit: punk preppy. Unfortunately I got some of the glitter eyeliner in my eye in third period. I raised my hand to ask Mr. MacIntosh if I could go to the nurse, and at that point I was in so much pain that I was almost crying. He said something that, with his Scottish accent, sounded to me like, "Boon in the doon moon." Gwennie reassured me that he said I could go and that she could help me.

Good thing too. My eyes were red and streaming, and I could barely make my way down the hall. Unfortunately I could see well enough to notice that Ashley was just getting dropped off at school as I was arriving at the nurse's office. I saw a look of wonder on her face. She was staring at

103

my red eyes, no doubt, and the fact that Gwennie was helping me walk.

I did make it back to class after cleaning out my contacts, but by then it was after lunch.

Tomorrow was January 30. My parents and Louanne would be at the dog show. Desperate times called for desperate measures. I had to go to London and find something absolutely fabulous to wear next Friday. And also, a wig for Hazelle.

# Chapter 25

"We're off, Savvy. Are you sure you'll be okay?" Mom asked as she slid her arms into her coat. Giggle was already tugging at his leash. He loved car rides and seemed to know, somehow, that this car ride was taking him to the last practice meet before the first competition Louanne had entered him into.

"I'll be fine." I avoided looking her in the eye.

"What will you do all day?" Dad asked. "Are you sure you don't want to come with us?"

"I'm going to . . . do some preparation work for my fashion shoot article," I said. While strictly the truth, it wasn't the whole truth. I was feeling a little sick to my stomach.

Mom checked her watch. "Oh! We've got to

get going. We'll be home in a few hours." They bundled out the door to the waiting car and tootled off down Cinnamon Street.

I sat on the couch for only a moment. I rationalized to myself that after all, they were taking a whole day to help Louanne with her dog training, but there had been no real promise—or even another mention—of taking me to London. And my article was very important.

I was fifteen. It was time to take matters into my own hands.

I ran upstairs and grabbed my mom's empty hobo purse, dumped my gear into it, and then zipped up my black boots. I was ready to go.

I had to wait at the corner only five minutes for the bus that scooted me to the nearby Underground terminal. I descended the stairway, bought a ticket, and waited for the Underground.

The railcars roared in front of me just seconds later. Last chance to change my mind. But I didn't. I got on.

We flew through the tunnels deep in the bowels of the city, and for some reason, it brought to mind Aunt Maude's sheep guts. I stared at the London Underground map in my hand. If I'd planned it right, I could take the Central Line right to Portobello Market and see if there were any cool, unusual fashions, then get on the Underground, go to Topshop—I'd always wanted to go there!—and then get right back on the Central Line and make it home. Ahead of my parents.

About a dozen stops later, we pulled up at Notting Hill Gate. I looked at my map. I had arrived.

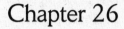

# Chapter 26

I got off the subway, enveloped by a huge group of strangers, all of whom seemed to be headed for the stairway to Portobello Road Market too. I found myself nose-to-armpit with a crowd of unwashed people. I could hardly hold my breath till I got to the top of the stairs, but with a few quick gasps of air I made it.

I burst into the winter sunshine and was greeted by block upon block of shops and street merchants. The air was heavy with the smell of kebabs cooking over kettle-can fires, roasted coffee beans, and unfiltered cigarette smoke. I pushed my way through the crowd toward the center of the long street. I couldn't see the end. I glanced at my watch. There was no way I would have time to make it all the way down one side and back if I was going to get to Topshop, too.

*Help me find the clothes section, Lord,* I reflexively prayed. I was surprised when I didn't sense anything back. Usually I felt His presence or direction, or even just companionship. But not now.

I hurriedly made my way down the row, looking at the tables as I went. There were antiques . . . and books and books and more books in the secondhand stalls. I could only imagine the number of Henry VIII books I might find there! But I pulled myself away. No leisure time for me today. I was in a hurry.

"Banana? Orange?" a snaggletoothed man asked me as I raced past a lovely fruit stand.

"No thank you," I said as I eyed the pomegranates. Louanne loved pomegranates, and so did I.

I saw a shop advertising hair products and wandered in.

"Hullo, luv," a matronly woman greeted me at the door. "How can I help you?"

"I'm looking for some hair clips and bands," I said. "Also . . . maybe do-it-yourself hair highlighting."

"Right here," she said approvingly. "I'm glad to have an average girl in here looking for highlights.

Not them fancy toffee girls. Don't believe in highlighting their hair now, do they? Well, says I, you've got to make the most of what you got."

I stopped her. "Oh . . . so high-class girls don't highlight their hair?"

She shook her head. "Not from what I've heard. Crazy, isn't it?" She shook her head from side to side, and the pink streaks in her black hair waggled with her. I had to admit, it was a little unsettling . . . seeing as she was Aunt Maude's age.

"How about some clips?" I said. She showed me to a display, and I picked out some tortoiseshell ones that I thought would look nice on Hazelle and a pure white headband that I thought would go well with my potential preppy-yachting style. Nothing classic rock. That would have to wait for Topshop. Speaking of which . . . "I'd better pay," I said. "I'm going to be late."

"Ten pounds, five p," she said, and I withdrew the exact amount from Mom's hobo purse and then tucked the bag back into it. I looked long-ingly up the road—it promised so many pleasures and fun things to explore. I'd seen a jelly pan my mom would like too. But how could I get it? Where would I tell her I'd bought it?

I shook my head. *Another day, I guess.* I headed

back to the Underground station, hoping to get to Topshop really quickly. I withdrew my day ticket, ran it through the slider in the Underground, and then put it with my purchases. I was on my way.

A few minutes later I emerged in front of Topshop. Just for a minute, I let it sink in all the way down to my toes. I was in London! At Topshop! I wished I could call Jen and tell her. Or maybe I should text Penny! It would be fun to share this with . . . well, anyone. A seed of regret settled in my heart and began to shoot tiny roots down into the soft flesh. I ignored it and marched into the store.

# Chapter 27

Sure, sure, I'd seen the slide shows on the Web site and checked out all the style guides online, assembling my dream outfits from their offerings. Of course I'd subscribed to their fashion podcasts and signed up for the style notes they sent out. But to actually be here!

Next to visiting the *Times* of London newspaper headquarters, and perhaps interviewing Henry VIII himself, this was the place above all places I wanted to be.

I checked my watch. I didn't have much time.

I ran to one floor and looked at some high-class dresses. Then I checked the price tags. Nope.

I flew to another department and sifted through the distressed jeans. I became a little distressed myself. Apparently I was going to have to be a really rich girl if I wanted to have the poor-girl look.

I passed the purses. No time to peruse today. Same with cosmetics. Finally I collapsed into a chair and looked around me.

I must have ended up in the sale section, because there were tables with items kind of scattered over the tops—neatly, of course, and with mannequins nearby, but still . . .

I stood up, walked over to a nearby table, and began to filter some of the fabrics through my fingers. I loved a scoop-necked peasant top in white and salmon. The gray lace cutout one with silver backing was cool too. I dared to peek at the price tags. Okay! I could afford both. I found a pair of jeans that had been stuffed under some sweaters. Just my size—and on sale, too. Someone had been hiding them there, I bet. Well, I found them.

I looked at my watch and felt panic rise. I had less than thirty minutes to make it back to the Underground in order to get home before my parents and Louanne. I grabbed a gold sweater off the sale table—only five pounds—thinking it would do something for Hazelle, and then I raced to the cashier. I glanced wistfully at the store map detailing the other departments. Did they have Dooney & Bourke in London? I didn't know. But I simply didn't have time to explore.

I walked out into the London rain and looked desperately at the street corners. Which one did I need in order to get to the right Underground station? I ran two blocks and hoped I would find the station I needed. When I got there, I pulled out my map and sighed with relief. It was the right one.

*Thank You, Lord,* I said as I descended the steps to the platform, stuffing everything into Mom's hobo purse except the Topshop bag. All the way back to Wexburg, my mind changed channels back and forth. First, I loved the two shirts and the jeans I'd bought and the sweater for Hazelle too. Topshop was everything I'd hoped it would be.

But somehow my pleasure in it was smaller than I'd thought it would be. Actually the whole day felt empty somehow. I hopped on the bus and after that walked really, really quickly down Cinnamon Street. I expected to see the car in the driveway.

# Chapter 28

In spite of my guilty conscience, the car wasn't in the driveway when I got home. It would be soon, though. Would they be able to tell by just seeing my face?

I ran into the house, took the stuff out of the Topshop bag, put the clothes away, and hung out in my room for a few minutes. It wasn't much longer before I heard the hum of our car and then the front door opening.

"Anyone home?" Mom called cheerily through the doorway.

I came down the stairs. "I'm here," I said. I looked at Louanne's flushed face. "How did it go?"

"Giggle did fantastic! I wish you'd have been there, Savvy," she said.

"Me too," I said, and you know, I kind of meant it. "I'll come next time. Promise."

She kicked off her boots, and Growl slowly padded to his water bowl, lapped for a good two minutes, then hauled himself to the one patch of sunlight on the living room floor and flopped down.

Dad fired up the computer right away, but Mom came over to talk with me. I was kind of surprised. "Yes?" I asked. Moms know everything.

"What do you mean, 'Yes?'" Mom asked. "I just wanted to spend some time with my daughter. I know I've been kind of busy lately. But this Wednesday is the library sale, and after that I'll have some more time. How about if I take you shopping on Friday night? Maybe to Topshop?"

I held my face really still. I wasn't sure if I should burst into tears or what. But if I told her the truth, she might get mad. Even worse, she might be really disappointed. Both because of my disobedience and because I'd spoiled our trip by taking matters into my own hands. It had seemed like such a good idea just a few hours ago. I didn't know what to do or what to say. So I just answered, "That would be really nice, Mom."

I leaned in and hugged her, and I wished, for

the first time, that she really *did* know everything. Because then she'd bring it up and save me this agony. Instead, she kissed the top of my head and went to take a nap.

Louanne brought down Monopoly, one of our favorite board games. "Want to play?" she asked hopefully.

"Sure," I said.

"Really?" she squealed. "I thought for sure you'd say no."

"Come on." I motioned her to the floor, and we set up the pieces. I took the top hat, as always, and she was the dog.

About ten minutes into the game, Growl heard a noise outside, leaped up from a dead sleep, and raced across the living room toward the front door, scattering the game pieces everywhere. "Oh no!" Louanne said, her eyes filling with tears. "Giggle, how could you?"

Unaccustomed to a sharp word from Louanne, Growl turned and looked at her. "You've ruined my game!" she shouted at him.

"It's all right," I said softly. "We can start over."

"But you were winning," Louanne said.

"I don't mind," I answered.

She looked up at me with the kind of little

sister adoration I hadn't seen in her for a long time. "Thank you, Savvy," she said. "I wish I were more like you."

I started resetting the game board. "No, you don't, Louanne," I said. "No, you really don't."

Later that night I pulled out some of the Asking for Trouble questions that Jack had given me. I needed to pick one for this coming week. I was almost afraid to look at them.

Most of them were typical—boyfriend trouble, girlfriend trouble, parent trouble. But one of them caught my eye right away. It was about a girl who had been cheating in school. She'd copied test questions. I knew that she'd be expelled from Wexburg Academy if they found out. There were severe consequences for cheating. I didn't think I really wanted to write a column about severe consequences and then learn all about them on my own.

I thumbed through my concordance, looking up the word *sin*. For the column, of course. I read through a few verses, most of which I was familiar with. My eyes and heart stopped when I read this:

You may be sure that your sin will find you out. NUMBERS 32:23

# Chapter 29

On Monday Hazelle and I sat next to each another at the newspaper lunch table. Penny was home sick—she'd texted me to tell me! Even though I was sorry she was sick, I felt really great that she'd let me know. Our friendship was definitely growing, and I hoped that nothing would derail it.

"Meet me at the newspaper office after school?" I asked Hazelle.

"Sure," she said. "Do you walk home?"

I nodded. "You?"

"Yes. A lot of them—" she jerked her thumb toward the Aristocat table—"get rides."

"I think most of their cars are too big to turn around on my street," I said, and Hazelle grinned. Actually, she was very pretty when she smiled.

Especially since her sandwich had mopped off most of her Ruby Desire lipstick.

We walked home in the drizzle. It's not like the conversation was easy, but it was okay and not silent. Since we both liked history, she told me about her dad's job at the British Museum. "Even though he's only a security guard, it's a very important position because of the value of the things he's guarding."

"What's your favorite thing there?" I asked.

"Room 40," she said without hesitation. My face must have shown my ignorance, because she followed it up with, "Medieval Europe."

"I think that sounds cool."

Just then we turned down Cinnamon Street and toward my house.

"'Kew Cottage,'" Hazelle read the plaque by the door.

I opened the door, and my mom met us just inside. "You must be Hazelle," she said warmly. "I'm Savvy's mom. I'm so glad you could come over."

*Please, please, Mom. Don't tell her that she's the first friend I've had over since we moved here.*

# Chapter 30

Mom took our jackets and hung them on the coat hanger right inside the hall. "I've made some snacks, if that's okay."

"Sure, I'm starved," Hazelle said.

I led the way into the kitchen and felt happy—and guilty—when I saw the nice spread my mom had set up for us. There was a bowl of fruit and some fizzy lemonade and a basket of chips—er, crisps—and a sour cream and chive dip to go with it. To the side was a little bowl of milk chocolate buttons. Hazelle took one and then another and then a third.

We took the snacks and headed to my room.

"Oh, you play the guitar?" She pointed to the guitar propped in the corner.

"Yes, when I can. I'm hoping to play at my church, maybe on Wednesday nights."

"You go to church? I don't think I know anyone who goes to church, really. Except for marrying and burying. And sometimes not even then." She took a large bite out of her apple. I noticed she didn't exactly close her mouth all the way when she chewed. I hoped she'd hold off on the snacks at the Peter Chen shoot.

"I thought if you wanted to, we could look through some of my fashion magazines." I pulled a big stack out from under my bed.

"Why?"

"This will help you get used to the terminology," I offered. "So you'll know an A-line from a pleat and all that before we go to the shoot and write up the article."

After taking another chomp out of her apple, she said, "Yeph. Phokey. Pantastic."

I think it was supposed to be "Yes. Okay. Fantastic." Without the mouthful of food. I hoped she didn't make a habit of talking with food in her mouth.

We paged through some of the magazines, and she actually took notes—which I thought was impressive—and then I launched into Operation HHH.

"What do you think of this style?" I asked, pointing out the smart librarian look, which I thought she had the most hope of achieving.

She shrugged. "It's fine, I suppose. But we won't really have any say at all in which kind of clothes they choose, right?"

"I . . . meant, you know, for you personally." My mom must have turned the heat up in the house. It was really stuffy in my room.

"Me? Oh no. I'm happy how I am."

I stood up and went to my closet, where I pulled out the sweater I'd bought with her in mind during the Topshop expedition. "I, uh, saw this when I was shopping and thought of you. I mean, the color is just right."

Hazelle reached for a chip and scooped some dip onto it. "That's kind of you, Savvy, but it's not really me."

"Maybe it could be you for one day . . . at the Chen shoot?"

"No *thanks*, Savvy," Hazelle said. I wandered over to the makeup I had on my dresser top and began rummaging for something. "What are you doing now?" she asked.

"Hunting for lipstick. I just noticed how much better I looked in a peach tone and thought maybe we could do makeovers on each other."

"Do you mean you want me to do your makeup . . . or you want to redo mine?" Hazelle said.

"Both!" I said as brightly as I could. "I just thought that the red you wear might be a shade too bright."

"Yes, and your earrings look like wind chimes."

I shook my head. They did jingle-jangle. They were a part of my Indian-look collection.

Hazelle stood up and checked her watch. "Savvy, I really appreciate your trying to bring me up to speed on this. But I think I know enough for how I'm going to write the piece, what angle I'm going to take. And honestly, not everyone wants to be one of your remodel projects."

I opened my mouth to protest that that's not at all what I'd been doing. But then I realized I *had* been doing that. I'd had enough dishonesty.

"Will you show me to the door?" she asked politely. "My mum will be expecting me soon."

I walked her downstairs. "See you in maths," I called after her. She smiled briefly, held up a hand, and waved good-bye.

I'd already closed the door when I realized that she'd said *she* was going to write the article and choose the angle. Over my dead body.

# Chapter 31

Monday night after Hazelle left, I paged through the Asking for Trouble questions. I thought I already knew the exact one I was going to use, and I prayed about it and felt certain that it was right, even though I didn't want it to be.

I looked up some verses that would help me craft the right answer. Time and again I was drawn to one passage: John 8:31-32. I knew this was the one I had to use. My heart was heavy.

*Lord, this isn't for the column, is it? I mean, it's for the column. But it's also for me, isn't it?*

I had questions for myself. Why had I done it? Who was I? Not the person I'd thought I was. And then the big question: what would I do? I needed some time to figure it out. *Not more than a week,* I promised the Lord . . . and myself.

I typed up my column, e-mailed it to Jack, and turned out the light. But I didn't sleep.

# Chapter 32

Penny was back at school the next day, and she approached me in PE. "Do you want to come over to my house next Monday after school?" She didn't exactly announce it to everyone . . . but she wasn't whispering, either.

"Yes!" I said. *Hooray!*

We trotted into the gym, and then our instructor, Miss Lashing, asked Chloe, her favorite, to divide us into groups. Chloe split the class up but put all of her friends on one team. Miss Lashing told Chloe to split us up again, so Chloe did, but she seemed distracted by having to do it over. She put Ashley in a group with only one other Aristocat—one I noticed was kind of klutzy. Then we took our sides to play floor hockey. The klutzy cat accidentally stuck her stick in front of Ashley, and Ashley fell. A quiet titter of laughter echoed through the gym. Ashley picked herself up slowly, brushed herself off, and glared to the north, to the south, to the east, and to the west. Then she went back to play.

At the end of the period, Ashley's team had lost—and lost badly. She confronted Chloe in the locker room, unplugging Chloe's straightener and plugging her own in its place—even though there was an open outlet.

"What was I to do, Ashley?" Chloe said. "It's not like I can jolly well tell the instructor what to do."

"No excuses." Ashley turned her back on her.

It was really clear to all of us what happened to anyone who made Ashley look bad.

# Chapter 33

That night, Tuesday, I studied really hard for the next day's science test, and when I was done, I had a brilliant idea. I was blonde, right? And nothing looks better on blondes than a little bronzing on their normally pale skin. I dug through a duffel bag I'd brought from the States and found exactly what I wanted. *Bronze Glo: For those in the know.*

I took a bath and shaved my legs first, then rubbed the rest of my skin with a washcloth to make sure there were no leftover skin flakes. I wanted a nice, even tan. I thought I'd just do a light coat at first, and then for Friday I'd add a little more. I knew I'd used this stuff before. I thought it had turned out okay. One thing I did remember, though—to wash my hands right after applying it. Otherwise your palms got "tan" too.

I smoothed the lotion all over my skin, stopping at my neck because I could put bronzer on my face. I washed my hands and let everything dry before getting into bed. Wednesday was going to be a good day.

Wednesday morning I woke up and, first thing, looked at my arm. Oh no! It wasn't bronze—it was orange. And not a little orange. Really orange. I looked like one of the Oompa-Loompas from Willy Wonka's chocolate factory. I ran from my bedroom, still in my pajamas, to find my mom.

"I can't go to school today. I'm not kidding. I really *am* sick." I held out my arm. I lifted a leg and held it up too.

"What happened to you?" Dad asked.

"Tanning lotion," Mom answered for me. "That's not sick."

"It sure looks sick," Dad said, grinning. He slunk away when I did not grin back.

"Get your uniform on. Wear tights. Keep your sleeves down today. Button your shirt to the neck, and wear your tie tight," Mom said.

I started to breathe again, just a little. Then I

remembered. "PE!" I practically shouted. I could see it now. I'd have to get shorts and a T-shirt on, and everyone would see my legs and arms. One of the Aristocats would point it out to Ashley, who would say, loudly, that she couldn't believe anyone would be that low class and she wasn't sure *at all* that I should come to the Peter Chen shoot. And then Penny would be embarrassed that she'd suggested me, and later she'd ask me to remove her number from my phone.

"Savvy!" Mom called out. "Did you hear me? Wear a sweat suit in PE today. It'll be okay."

"Oh, oh yeah. Good idea, Mom."

She came over and kissed my head, and I pulled away. She looked startled but said nothing. I, of course, couldn't tell her that I really wanted us to be tight again, but with the secret disobedience between us, I felt unworthy.

I got dressed and went to school. I even made it all the way through PE by changing in a bathroom stall. And then I went to science.

We took our seats—mine next to Gwennie and Jill—and Mr. MacIntosh passed out the tests. I nearly chewed off the end of my pencil thinking, which was a trick indeed because it was a mechanical pencil. But I thought I did well.

As soon as he'd collected the tests, Mr. MacIntosh said something odd. Even with his accent, I was sure he said, "I'd like everyone in the classroom to remove your jackets and roll up your sleeves if you have long sleeves on."

*What? Roll up my sleeves? Today?* I leaned over to Gwennie. "What's going on?"

She shrugged and rolled up her sleeves, revealing her smooth, black forearms.

I raised my hand. "Excuse me, sir," I said, trying the extra-respectful angle. "I'm just wondering why we're doing this."

"Certainly, Miss Smith." He rolled the *r* in his thick Scots accent. He moved closer to me. Oh, great. By asking a question, I'd drawn every eye in the class on me. He kept talking while indicating that I should roll up my sleeves.

"There have been some reports of cheating at Wexburg Academy. In fact, there have been several reports of students writing answers—theorems, concepts—on their arms before taking tests. I'm certain that no one in my class has done that. But I'd best be making sure. You've got nothing to hide, eh, lassie?"

Well, actually I did, but it wasn't science notes. I began rolling back my sleeves. The bright orange looked neon when contrasted with the bleached white of my uniform top. No kidding, I heard at least four gasps in the room. I showed him that, while orange, my arms had no words written on them. He nodded and moved on. I looked no one in the eye.

After class Gwennie held my arm to talk for a minute. We stayed in our seats. "What happened to you?" she asked. "Did you fall into a bowl of cheesy puffs?"

I grinned. "Uh, I eat a lot of carrots and mangoes . . . ?"

She shook her head. "Nice try. It's tanning lotion, isn't it?"

I nodded. "Yeah."

"Savvy," she said, "what's going on?"

I sighed. "I'm trying to . . . make the most of what I've got. You know—be all that I can be. Actually—" I hung my head a little—"I'm not sure at all who I am anymore."

She laughed out loud. "Sure you do. And I do too. I like her. I'm just not sure about the orange girl." She stood, her black braids swinging. "See you later. Maybe at Fishcotecque. Okay?" She ran to catch up with Jill.

I thought about the students who had been

cheating. I thought about the Asking for Trouble column I'd answered. It would be out first thing tomorrow morning.

# Chapter 34

I got to school early on Thursday, as always, to deliver the paper. By the time I went back to fill up my Au Revoir bag (which now had a small hole in the bottom) for the second time, I saw people all over campus reading the paper. Their low-voiced discussions hummed all across the grounds.

Jack grinned at me when I came back into the office before heading to maths. "A lot of talk about the Asking for Trouble column today, eh, Savvy?"

He didn't say anything at all to give away our secret. Just pleasant conversation.

"I'll say," Hazelle said. "Wish I knew who wrote it!"

I heard little snippets of conversation all day about the column, which was . . . weird. I mean, I know it was getting to be popular, but still, I never expected people to talk about it all day. I wondered what was going on but didn't want to seem overly interested.

After school I went around the paper distribution centers on campus and picked up the few copies that were left. One of the spots, near the gym, had a small stack. I took them, tucked all but one into the Au Revoir bag, and sat down on a bench. Then I read the column in print for the first time.

**D**ear Asking for Trouble, I missed quite a few days of school due to illness. I just wasn't feeling myself, even after I got better, and I couldn't catch up. So I cheated on a few things. I used some cheat notes for a test and also had a friend help me write a paper because I felt so far behind. My parents get really angry when my grades aren't top notch. I don't feel good about it, but no one seems to know, and now the crisis has passed. I'm on top of my grades again. But I don't feel right. What should I do?

Sincerely,
*An "A" Student Once Again*

❤

**D**ear **"A,"** I'm sorry you were ill and that you had some problems to deal with afterward. Doesn't seem fair, does it? But the problem with trying to fix things through deception, as you've found out, is that even if no one else knows, you know. You sound like a nice person, so I'm betting that you didn't want to cheat the school, your friends, and yourself by taking the wrong path. Wouldn't it be nice to have a good night's sleep again? There's a wise saying: the truth will set you free. Because even if you haven't been caught, you're still trapped. Fess up. Be free.

Honestly yours,
*Asking for Trouble*

What was honest about trying to change my style to meet what I thought would impress the

Aristocats? Because, for all of my excuses, that was the truth of it. I was not a vegan. I loved bacon and deep-fried fish. And if it weren't bad enough that I was trying to change myself, I was trying to change other people, too. For example, Hazelle. I sat there, sighed, and closed my eyes.

Would the real Savvy Smith please step forward?

In a minute, I felt someone slide onto the bench next to me. I opened my eyes.

"Hullo," he said. "You all right?"

I nodded. I must have looked odd sitting on the bench, clutching a newspaper, with my eyes closed.

"Good column, that," he said. "Heard that the girl turned herself in to the headmaster today. He went easier on her because she confessed."

"Really?" I asked. Now I was wide awake.

"Really," the boy answered. "Pretty powerful writing. You were right, you know."

*What?* He couldn't possibly know I'd written this column. I didn't even know him. "What do you mean?" I asked carefully.

"Don't you remember?" he asked. "You told me a few months ago that I should read the school paper more often. And I have been."

I searched my memory for him. Brown hair, cute brown eyes. I smiled. Now I remembered. "I was interviewing people to see if they read the paper."

"Yes. Pleased to see I made such a strong impression. You made a strong impression on me, though."

I blushed and was glad that my long sleeves were still rolled down, covering up Agent Orange.

"What's your name?" he asked as he stood up and slung his brown leather backpack over one shoulder.

"Savvy, uh, Savannah," I said.

"Mine's Tommy," he said. "See you around, *Savvy, uh, Savannah*. Maybe at a dog show." He grinned and waved.

I offered a smile and a weak wave in return. My stomach did a little flip as he turned and walked away.

Yes! Of course! That's where I'd seen him. He'd waved to me at the dog show before Christmas.

He'd recognized me then, too.

I folded up the paper and started walking back to the newspaper staff office. I should be thrilled—elated! I'd asked the Lord to help me do good for

Him, and my column had done just that. Someone had done the right thing because of what I'd written. At least one person, maybe more.

But one person had not done the right thing. I would, though. I had to get back to being the real, true, honest Savannah Smith, aka Savvy. Whose skin was pale, who wore bohemian fashionista put-together outfits, who liked history and loathed math. Who fessed up when she'd done wrong.

This last one would have to come about after Monday though, because I couldn't be grounded from Penny's.

# Chapter 35

The next day was casual Friday—no uniforms. I wore the jeans and peasant blouse I'd found at Topshop and pulled my hair back into a messy ponytail. I didn't wear much makeup but slicked on a light gloss. The orange—thankfully—was almost gone from my skin.

"You look lovely!" Mom said as I got ready to leave. "I don't remember that shirt. But then, I can hardly keep track of my own clothes! Say, I owe you some shopping. Do you want to go tonight? We can find something for you to wear to that photo shoot!"

"Oh, um, no thanks," I said. I felt so bad. She was being so nice.

"Oh, Sav, I'm sorry it's taken me so long to

take you. I really am," Mom said. "But let's go, okay? I've been looking forward to it. And you can buy something for Louanne—we're having her birthday dinner tomorrow night, you know."

I nodded. I didn't want to disappoint her, and I did need to find something for my sister.

Everyone loved my outfit that day. Gwennie gave me a big thumbs-up in science. "Now *that's* my Savvy," she said. "Back to her own free-flowing style."

At lunch Penny waved me over to sit next to her.

Ashley spoke up. "I love that shirt," she said to me. Everyone looked at me, gaping. When Ashley complimented your clothes, you knew you'd scored.

But somehow I just wanted to pull my coat on. Guilt and deception did not make good accessories.

# Chapter 36

Mom and I took off that afternoon for London. Stores here didn't stay open as late as in the States, so we left early and planned to have dinner at the Eat café.

"Have fun, girls!" Dad called after us.

I promised myself I would, if not for me, then for Mom. We zipped down Cinnamon Street and toward London.

"I'm so excited that you're making good friends," Mom said. "Hazelle over this week, then going to Penny's house on Monday. I was worried about you for a while. But things are looking up. They both seem nice, too."

"Penny is," I said, picking at my nail polish. "And, well, I guess Hazelle is too. In her own way."

"Tell me about the fashion shoot," Mom said. "It's easier for me to listen than talk since I'm driving on the wrong side of the road."

For a while I forgot about my trip downtown—I was just so glad to have some one-on-one time with Mom again. We got to Topshop, and I fell in with her excitement, except I had to add to the deception a little when she said, "Isn't it fun for us to be here together for the first time?"

I smiled but didn't answer. I knew that was a lie of its own, though.

We found an extremely cute leggings set for Louanne and got it gift-wrapped. "Want to try the nail bar?" Mom held out her slightly bitten fingernails.

I shook my head. "Maybe we can come back before the fashion shoot?"

"Great idea!" Mom said. "Let's go find your outfit."

We browsed through several departments, and I settled on a creamy white knit skirt with a funky sweater and fuzzy tights. Some brown suede shoes with a strap and a chunky heel rounded it off.

"I don't even mind spending the money,"

Mom said as she paid. "You've been patient—both for shopping and for the article. It's worth it."

# Chapter 37

The next day we brought Louanne breakfast in bed—chocolate chip pancakes, her favorite. That afternoon she had a party with her school friends. She introduced me to each of them, one by one. "This is my big sister, Savvy. She's a journalist, you know."

"Oh, fantastic," the girls would say one after the other. It felt nice to be a big sister and to have her be so proud of me. It made me want to set a good example for her to follow. I'd put a bow tie on Growl, and he must have sensed that this was a special day for Louanne, because he stood still for it.

Twelve cupcakes served, twelve presents opened, four party games played, and then the girls went home. Louanne went to take a nap before we went to Beet and Potato, a vegetarian restaurant, for dinner. I made her two gift certificates—my big gifts for her, because I knew they were the things she wanted most.

GIFT CERTIFICATE

This certificate is good for one fabulous big sister/ little sister date to none other than Fishcatege— formerly known as my private hangout, now open to you, too. I'll have fish; we'll both have chips and Fanta. You can keep the mushy peas to yourself!

XOXO

GIFT CERTIFICATE

This certificate is good for your own personal photojournalist for a day—ME!—ready to capture Growls—oh, I mean Giggles's— best side, I know he has one! I promise to find it! Then you can send your pix back to all our friends and family in Seattle and show them what you're up to. They're going to be so surprised!

XOXO,
Savvy

My parents were pretty cool and had a lot of good qualities, but picture taking wasn't one of them. My dad cut off everyone's heads in pictures— I called him Henry VIII—and Mom tended to be way off center.

After wrapping the gift certificates, I cleaned

up the living room. A ball of wrapping paper had rolled under the couch, and I reached in to get it. When I did, I felt something else and pulled it out too.

A Get Out of Jail Free card from last week's Monopoly game. It must have flown there when Growl did his damage.

I looked at it a long time, and the Holy Spirit brought back to my mind the passage I'd used in my latest column, John 8:31-32. I would never, ever, have guessed that I'd say this, but I couldn't wait till Monday night so I could confess. I only hoped that nothing would happen between now and then to mess it up. Two days.

Later that night, after we'd all feasted—if one can use such a word when only veggies are involved—I settled into bed to read for a few minutes before turning off my light.

A gentle knock came at the door.

"Who is it?"

"It's me, Sav. Louanne."

"Come on in," I said, dog-earring the page of my book before closing it.

Louanne walked into my room and plopped on the bed beside me, calves and feet dangling over the side. Growl waggled in after her, refusing to look at me, of course, but plopping down at Louanne's feet.

"Thanks for the gift certificates," she said. "Especially the one about taking pictures."

I breathed a sigh of relief. "Actually, I was hoping you wouldn't think they were lame. I mean, I could have bought you some books or gotten you a gift card for music or something."

"The one to come and take pictures of me and Giggle is actually my favorite," she said.

I was going to leap in with a comment, but something told me to let her keep talking when she would.

"I mean, everyone back home can see that you've got something really special here, you know, with the paper and all. I'm really excited to send them some good pictures of me and Giggle at the dog show. So they can see that, you know, I have important activities too." She looked up at me. "It's fun having a big sister, but sometimes people pay most attention to the oldest in the family and kind of forget the things the younger ones do."

Her little face was so earnest, so grown up, that it broke my heart. "I don't ever forget that *you* and whatever you do are important," I said.

Louanne grinned and made a funny face at me that told me she wasn't buying it.

"Okay, not *mostly*," I said. Then we both laughed.

"Good night, big sister." She jumped off the bed.

"Happy birthday, little sister," I replied.

On their way out the door, Growl turned and gave me a rare look of approval.

I went back to my book, satisfied. How easy it had been to make her happy.

For a minute, but not much longer, it made me forget Monday and the confession I had to make.

I dove back into my book and its fantasy life to forget my real life, if only for an hour.

# Chapter 38

"Ready, then?" Penny met me outside the gym at the end of the day on Monday.

"Ready." We began walking toward the front of the school. I saw a couple of chauffeurs out there waiting for some of the students—mostly Aristocats, as Hazelle had said. But I didn't see Penny's mom's zippy little sports car. "Is your mom here yet?" I asked politely.

Penny looked puzzled. "Oh, she's not coming. We'll walk."

I smiled. Penny was definitely different from her friends. Well, that's what I thought till we walked in front of her row house. No, it wasn't The Beeches, exactly. But it wasn't Kew Cottage, either. She punched in a code, and two big metal

159

gates silently swung open. There was a large bronze plaque that said, "Hill House."

Once inside the gates, Penny punched a code into another box, and we began walking up her long driveway. As we did, two Irish setters came racing to meet, greet, and lick us. She looked at me. "Do you like dogs?"

"We have one," I said drily. Was this country ruled by dog lovers?

Her house was large but tasteful. She opened her own door—no butler here. The floors were polished to a high gloss, and there was a lot of classy furniture decked out in chintz and arrangements of fresh flowers. My mother hardly ever bought fresh flowers. She said plants lasted longer.

Penny dropped her book bag by the front door—just like me!—and we walked toward the kitchen.

"Hullo, Mum. This is Savvy." She kissed her mother on each cheek, and her mother did likewise.

"Hello, Savvy. How do you do?"

Aha. I was ready for this one. My handy-dandy *Guide to London for Outsiders* informed me that this was not a question but a comment, and I was to answer with the same.

"How do you do?" I responded. I noticed a faint upturn in her mother's mouth. I'd passed!

"Delighted to meet you," she said. "Penelope, I've had Stella set out some snacks. I'm going to my book club meeting, but I'll be back before dinner. Will you need a ride home, Savvy?"

"No thank you," I said. "My mother will be here in a few hours to pick me up."

"Fine," her mother said. "Then I'll leave the gates open when I go and I'll have Stella bring the dogs inside."

A book club! Just like my mom. Maybe they'd be friends someday. Penny and I grabbed a stack of snacks and headed up to her room. I couldn't help but notice that the entire top floor of Kew Cottage would have fit inside her bedroom.

We sat cross-legged on her four-poster and ate chips with dip on porcelain plates and a lot of other yummy, non-Aristocat-approved snacks. "Penelope, huh?" I teased.

"Yes, I know," she said. "Mothers. I suppose yours calls you Savannah."

"Only when I'm in trouble," I admitted.

She reached over and, using a remote control, clicked on some music that came from hidden speakers in her room. British techno-pop.

Girl rock. I loved it—we shared the same taste in music.

"So, tell me all about yourself and your family. Why did you move here? How long will you stay?"

I told her all about my life both in Seattle and here. I didn't mention my secret column for the WA *Times*, of course, but I did say I hoped to become a journalist. "Jack and Melissa have both been really kind since I've been here," I said.

"Do they do everything as a couple?" she asked with a laugh.

It caught me off guard. "Are they a couple?" I asked. I hadn't noticed.

She must have seen the look in my eye. "Oh, well, I'm not sure. I'm sure you'd know better than I do." I was glad I hadn't mentioned my little crush on Union Jack.

"Melissa seems really fantastic," she said. "I'm glad she's coming to the fashion shoot."

I took a deep breath. I couldn't believe I hadn't told her yet. "Uh, Penny, I have something to tell you about that."

# Chapter 39

"I wanted to invite Melissa," I said, "but Jack had apparently promised the next assignment to Hazelle. So she's coming instead. But I'm in charge of the piece totally, and I'll make sure Hazelle stays in line at the shoot too."

My stomach did a little lurch at that. I hadn't had a lot of success controlling Hazelle.

Penny finished chewing a bit of her brownie, looked at me thoughtfully, and then said, "Well, all right. But you'll make sure that The Beeches and Ashley's family are portrayed positively, right? Because it seems Hazelle doesn't like Ashley too much."

"It'll be just fine," I said firmly. "Don't worry."

She smiled and finished the rest of her brownie.

I told her about my disastrous attempt at giving Hazelle a makeover last week. "It didn't work because, well, she wanted to be herself," I said.

"I'm glad you were back to your own self last Friday too," Penny said. "No more fake-bake tan."

I blushed. "You noticed."

She nodded. "But . . . I would like you to think about giving me a makeover."

I held up my hand like a stop sign. "Oh no," I said. "I've learned—or learnt, as you Brits would say—my lesson on that."

"This is different," Penny said. "Hazelle didn't want your help. I do."

I sipped my iced tea. "What do you mean?"

"I just . . . I don't know. I mean, I like my friends and all that—we've been friends forever— but sometimes I feel like I'm exactly the same as them on the outside when inside I'm not. I guess I want my outside to be a bit more like my inside. And to be different, just a little noticeable somehow. So I don't disappear."

I nodded thoughtfully. "Like at Ashley's house. She sat on a chair that was the same fabric as the drapes behind her. When she stood up, the one disappeared into the other."

"Exactly." Penny crunched on a crisp for effect.

"First," I said, "we'll start with dyeing and high-lighting your hair."

Penny's crisp dropped, and she looked panicked.

I laughed. "I'm kidding, of course." I remembered the lady at Portobello Road telling me that upper-class British girls didn't color their hair. "But hair is a good place to start, because you can do something different right away."

I scooted over near her. "What kind of look are you going for?"

Penny sat there and thought. "Nothing too . . . wild. But nothing too . . . dull, either. Something a bit less, um, controlled?"

I bit my lip, nodded, and then got to work braiding her hair on either side of her face, then asked her for a ponytail holder. She didn't have one—just a strip of ribbon—so I used that to loosely tie them in the back.

She got up and looked in the mirror. "My hair is so thin," she complained.

It wasn't exactly thin, but it could use a little poufing. I showed her the trick I'd discovered of adding face powder to the base of your hair and then combing it backward and giving just the tiniest spritz of hair spray.

"Wow! It's much thicker," she agreed. "It looks better."

I grinned and agreed. "I like your hair both ways. You're stylish through thick *and* thin," I said. "Now, let's try something else." I pulled her hair back again but did it just a bit different this time.

"I like it," she said. "It's not hippie chick, but it is . . ."

"Freer," I finished for her. "That's what we're going for. Free Penny!"

She laughed, and I agreed to bring some of my magazines to school so we could look over them together. And then, because she'd been so honest with me and because I'd been desperate for a real, true friend to confide in, I fessed up. My coach was about to turn into a pumpkin.

"My mom will be here soon," I said. "And I'm not looking forward to it."

"Why not? I thought you were close with your parents."

"I am," I said. I proceeded to tell her the whole story about the Underground trip and Topshop and how I had to come clean.

"Like that girl who was cheating at school and came clean after the Asking for Trouble column," Penny said.

"Exactly." *More so than you'll ever know.*

"Don't worry," she said. And then with a wicked grin and a reference to one of our favorite subjects, she said, "What can they do to you, anyway? Lop off your head?"

"My dad has been known to do that," I said, and she looked startled. I suppose I should have told her I meant in photographs.

# Chapter 40

As soon as I got into the car, I knew something was wrong. The air just felt stifled. Penny waved good-bye to me from the stairs in front of her row house. I pasted on a smile and waved back. Then I turned to my mother, who was emanating an evil vibe.

"I had a good time," I said.

"That's nice."

"Her house is nice, and I think you'd like her mom."

"Oh."

Nothing more was said for the quarter of a mile we drove down the road, and then we got stuck in backed-up traffic at a roundabout. I sighed. No time like the present. "I have something to tell you," I said. "Something you're not going to like."

"I know," Mom said.

"You know what?" My heart swelled in my chest, and I felt my head go light.

"I know you have something to tell me, and you're right, I don't like it. But save it till we get home. Dad is waiting there, and we'll talk when we're all together."

*She knew. But how?*

I should have jumped out of the car, since we were stopped anyway, and run away from home. I had only about ten pounds in my purse, though, so that wasn't going to get me very far.

We drove the rest of the way, parked the car, and mounted the steps. When I opened the door, Growl and Louanne were nowhere to be found, but my dad was sitting on the couch with a very sour expression.

I had the feeling I was about to meet the grim reaper.

# Chapter 41

"Have a seat," Dad said.

Who was I to disobey? Well, um, let me rethink that. In any case, I sat down on the chair and let them sit together on the couch—a good, safe six feet away from me.

"Savannah said she has something to tell us," Mom said. "I think we should let her speak."

Dad nodded, so I started in. "Well, see, I was really worried about what I was going to wear at the fashion shoot on the twentieth. So since everyone was busy, I thought it would be okay if I took the Underground—which is very safe, as you know—and went shopping for just a few hours."

"On Saturday the thirtieth," Mom said.

I nodded. "How did you know?"

She held up her purse—the hobo purse I'd borrowed the day I'd gone to London. "You left the Underground ticket in the bottom of my purse."

Oh. Yes. *"Be sure that your sin will find you out."*

"I'm really sorry," I said. "But on the other hand, you guys haven't had any time for me lately, really, and this is very important to me."

"Don't blame us for this," Dad bellowed, and I shrank into the chair.

After a minute, I spoke up again. "I'm not blaming you. I'm very sorry, and I take full responsibility for it. But you have been busy with work, and Mom with her book club sale, and everyone with the dog show. And honestly, I just didn't know if the London trip was even going to happen or if it was a 'we'll see' kind of thing that no one thought about again. Like Wednesday night church." I started sniffling and tried, hard, to will the tears to stay trembling at the edge of my eyelashes, but they spilled down anyway. "This hasn't been the easiest year of my life, you know."

I got all that out in nearly one breath and then let my shoulders fall.

"Why didn't you tell us before?" Mom asked. "Looking back, I can see how bad you felt. You've been unhappy and hanging out in your room more. You didn't even enjoy Topshop as much as I thought you would."

"That's true," I agreed. "Well, I just didn't want you to ground me from going to Penny's today. I planned to tell you afterward. I wanted one friend. Is that so bad?"

"No," Dad agreed. "But I'm very disappointed, Savannah, in how you went about this." The clock ticked for a few moments. "On the other hand, I do understand. We have been very busy. And perhaps we overlooked a few things. Your mom and I will talk about that. We'd already decided you'd be grounded, but perhaps, considering the circumstances, you can be grounded for one week instead of two."

"If you'd have told us up front, we may not have grounded you at all," Mom said.

My mind raced back to the girl who'd admitted after the Asking for Trouble column that she'd been cheating. She was disciplined, but because she'd come forward, she wasn't expelled.

"All right," I said.

"Come here." Mom patted the couch between her and Dad. I sat beside them, and they each put an arm around me. "You talk more, and I'll listen more, okay?"

I sniffed and nodded.

"Your grounding can start tonight," Dad said. "To school and back, nothing else. No phone calls, no going anywhere. House only. But then you'll be done before the twentieth, which is your fashion shoot day, right?"

"Yes." I sensed, more than heard, Louanne at the top of the steps. I heard Growl panting as she held him by his collar, probably practically strangling him. She was listening. I suddenly remembered. "Louanne's dog show is this Saturday!" I said.

"There'll be other ones," Mom said.

"No, no, I promised her this one," I said. "It's her first big show. She wants me to take pictures to send to Seattle so she can show her friends. I told her I would."

Now I heard Louanne's loud breathing from the top of the stairs, right along with Growl's.

"Well, we'll let you make the choice. You can start your grounding today or next Sunday, right after the dog show."

"If I do the dog show, I'll miss the Peter Chen shoot!"

Mom looked at Dad, and they both nodded. "Actions have consequences, Savvy. Let us know tonight what you want to do."

I headed to the stairs, and as I did, I heard Louanne scamper out of the way, the door to her room closing before I got to the top. I opened my own door, entered my room, and sat down on my bed.

If I'd confessed one day earlier, I might not have been grounded at all. It reminded me of something a teacher had told me long ago. "The time to do the right thing is as soon as you become aware that it's the right thing to do."

What should I do? On one hand, if I waited till next week to start the grounding, I could go to Louanne's dog show. I'd promised her—it was her birthday present, for heaven's sake. She looked up to me. And like my parents had been too busy for me lately, I'd been too busy for her.

On the other hand, this shoot was my chance at a column of my own. About a topic I loved. Most important, Penny had scored the tickets for me, and I had a responsibility to her to make sure it went well. If I didn't go to the shoot, Hazelle would be in charge of the article. And who knows what she might say? Then where would Penny be? And where would our friendship be? If there was one left at all.

I sat there thinking. Actually, my mother had

given me the answer. And Louanne had heard her say it. *"There'll be other ones,"* Mom had said. And of course, she was right. There would be other shows, but there would not be other fashion shoots. There might not be other friends either if Hazelle burned Ashley (and Penny). Louanne would understand. I'd make it up to her and she would get that I was not sacrificing her and her interests.

That settled, I breathed a sigh of relief and headed toward my desk to do some homework.

I opened my French notebook, and as I began to study the phrases, a light knock came on my door. "Who is it?"

"Me." Louanne's voice squeaked through the crack in the door.

"Come in."

She came alone, without Growl, and sat on my bed. "I'm sorry about what happened," she said.

"Me too. Now you know why I said you didn't want to be like me."

"Everyone makes mistakes, Savvy. I still want to be like you. And it's okay if you skip my dog show."

I looked down at her, so sweet, so willing to give up something very important to her—for me.

"You know what, Louanne? I think *I* want to be like *you*."

When she left, I opened my closet door and looked at the soft white knit skirt, funky sweater, and supercool blocky brown shoes I'd planned to wear to the show. Peter Chen would love them. And so would Ashley. I closed the closet door.

*"There'll be other ones,"* Mom had said, and I reminded myself of it over and over again. Louanne could hardly hold it against me if Mom had suggested it, right? And Louanne had *heard* her suggest it, so it wouldn't even seem like I was dodging responsibility. And after Louanne's sweet visit, I knew she wouldn't hold it against me.

I brushed my teeth, said good night, and got into bed. I tossed. And turned. I rolled over and over so many times I felt like a rotisserie chicken. Then I got out of bed.

"Might as well study if I'm not going to sleep," I grumbled. I headed back to my French notebook.

I memorized a few phrases and determinedly drew a line through them when I had them mastered. Then I came to the second-to-last phrase, *bon courage.* "It means something like 'good luck,' but not exactly," the definition read. "Perhaps it's similar to 'take heart' or 'be courageous'—something you might wish someone who is embarking upon a difficult but righteous journey or undertaking."

I said it again and again in my head, memorizing it. *Bon courage, bon courage, bon courage.*

I drew a weak line through the phrase and switched off my desk lamp. In the dark, I quietly opened my closet door and looked at my photo shoot outfit. Then I went back to bed with the words still flowing through my mind.

*Bon courage.*

# Chapter 42

I got to the newspaper room early the next morning—it was Tuesday, so I knew Jack would be in there early getting things going.

"Jack, can we talk for a second?"

He set down the article he was reading. "Sure, what's up?"

*Bon courage,* I told myself, trying to convince my eyes to dry and my mouth to smile. "I'm not going to be able to cover the Peter Chen fashion shoot."

"Why not? You've been looking forward to that for a month. And it's your chance to have your . . . actual name on the article."

"Trouble at home. But listen. I do have two tickets." I quickly prayed and hoped that the plan I'd cooked up on the way to school would fly. "Can I give mine to Melissa? She could take my place and be in charge of the shoot and all?"

Just then a few of the staff started to filter into the office—Rodney and one of the other reporters.

Jack shook his head. "Melissa will be gone that weekend. Away with her family, I'm afraid." He sure knew a lot about her personal life. "No, Savvy, I'm sorry. At this point, what I have to say is that Hazelle is going to be in charge of the Peter Chen photo shoot. Maybe you can help her with the edits afterward."

I squeezed my eyes shut to keep away any possibility of tears, and when I opened them, Hazelle was standing right behind Jack.

"Something I ought to know?" she asked.

"Later, yes," Jack said. "But right now I've got to finish up this week's copy."

I slid out the door and made it to first period. I sat on the opposite side of Brian, far enough away from Hazelle's seat that we couldn't talk.

We had an assembly during second period, and then there was a mandatory newspaper meeting at lunch, so I didn't see Penny till history class.

I got there early. I'd learned my lesson about waiting to share bad news.

"Hullo, Savvy," she said. She'd done her hair in the loose kinda-hippie braids I'd shown her how to do the day before.

"Hey, Penny," I said. I reached into my book bag and withdrew a large envelope. "I cut out some pictures from my fashion magazines to show you a few styles I was thinking of for you. Kind of high-class gypsy. Or upper-crust free spirit. You know, to fit in with your love of art."

"Thank you!" Her eyes shone as she reached for the envelope. I hated to dim them. But I had to.

"But . . . I have bad news," I said.

"Your parents?" she guessed.

I nodded. "I'm grounded. During the Peter Chen fashion shoot."

Her face fell. "Oh no. Oh no for several reasons. First, I'm sorry for you. And then . . . I'm sorry for me. But you couldn't help it. I mean, they grounded you."

"I'm so sorry, Penny. I can ask Jack to cancel the whole idea."

It was my last idea. But it could work.

Penny shook her head. "No. Mum has already

told Lady Gorm Strauss, and she told her friends from the Wexburg Academy Foundation. Who is going to be in charge of the article, then?"

"Hazelle," I whispered.

She looked away.

# Chapter 43

The next day Penny and I made awkward conversation in PE, but it was clear that she was still an Aristocat, and when Chloe picked her for a team, she went with her without a glance back at me.

"Don't worry about a thing," Gwennie said to me. "Jill and I were hoping you'd be on our team."

"Thanks, Gwennie," I said. She was a good pal. But I missed what I thought I could have had with Penny, too. Then again, if that's all it took for her to decide we weren't friends, maybe she wasn't a friend after all.

At lunch Penny sat at her Aristocat table, and Hazelle had her back turned to me, talking with one of her friends from the Agricultural Society.

I walked past her to spend lunch in the library, and as I did, I overheard her tell her friends that the fashion shoot article had been "reassigned" to her. Her voice sounded smug.

"Whatever do you want to do a fashion article for?" her friend asked, and they laughed. Things did not look good.

♥

The next morning, as Hazelle and I were loading my Au Revoir bag with papers, I decided to talk to her about the article.

"Hazelle, I want to apologize to you," I started.

She practically dropped her load of papers. "Why?"

"For trying to make you over. I was only trying to help. And you know, make you comfortable for the fashion shoot."

"Thanks for the apology, Savvy, but I'm perfectly comfortable doing any article. And it will be my name on the byline now."

*Rub a little salt in that bleeding wound, Hazelle.* My first impulse was to throw the stack of papers at her. But Penny was at stake.

"Yes, I know your name will be on the byline," I said, slipping another stack of papers into my bag. "But I hope you'll be . . . gracious . . . in your treatment of The Beeches and the Gorm Strausses since, you know, you're their guest."

"I don't need you telling me how to dress, how to act, or what to write," Hazelle said. "Here's the last stack of papers. Time to deliver them."

# Chapter 44

On Friday I wore the second shirt I'd bought on my ill-fated Topshop trip. Now that it was out in the open, though, I didn't feel so bad about wearing it. In PE Penny smiled encouragingly at me from across the gym. I waved a little at her.

At lunch I could see Penny's outfit. It was based on one of the styles I'd cut out of the magazine. She smiled at me as I passed the lunch table. "Like it?" she asked. Her hair was in the tied-back braids. It was a peace offering to our friendship, and I knew it.

"Love it," I said. "Can I sit here?"

"Sure," she said. She bit into an "unapproved" brownie.

I looked around. Everyone else at the table

had straight, no-nonsense hair. Some of them took a glance at Penny's gently original hairstyle now and then, though they didn't comment. She pretended not to see them glancing over, but I knew she did. I smiled at her for support.

Ashley said nothing.

# Chapter 45

Louanne and I got up early the next morning, Saturday, the day of the dog show. Dad snorted down his tomato juice with hot sauce and then jangled the car keys. "Ready to go?"

"Ready," I said.

Louanne was in the bathroom pleading with the dog. "Giggle! Sit still. I have to finish combing you. Savvy, help!"

I went into the bathroom and held the dog still while Louanne ran a comb through him, smoothing down his fur with Dr. Ruff's organic fur-smoothing cream. "Oh, Louanne. He's been passing gas in here," I said, gagging.

"Sorry. Nerves," she said. A minute later she looked at him. "He's ready."

We tumbled into the car, and Dad started it up. Mom waved from the driveway. I knew she wanted to come with us but was leaving Louanne and me to ourselves. Sisterly bonding, you know.

We pulled up to a green field that had a plastic banner over it that read *Kent Youth Dog Showmanship—Welcome All*. Dad dropped us off with strict instructions not to leave the field under any circumstances and to text him when we were ready to come home.

Growl looked like he was going to throw up. Louanne did too. It was my job to cheer them up.

"Come on," I teased. "Isn't it better to have me here than Aunt Maude?"

"Yes." Louanne giggled. "She kept flirting with the old-men judges."

"Really?" I was shocked. I didn't know she had it in her. We registered and got Growl a number.

"Ladies and gentlemen, young ladies and gentlemen, canines of all breeds and ages, if I may have your attention, please," the barker came over the loudspeaker. "Please make your way to the ring, where the competition will begin."

Louanne was clearly the youngest competitor there. Growl watered the bushes nearby while we waited, to the dismay of a woman in a large gray hat. She noted his number on a pad. I hoped she wasn't a judge.

When it was Louanne's turn, she had to make sure Growl walked at a pace just at her heels, didn't go too fast or too slow, and wasn't distracted. He had to walk down and back and then in a triangle pattern. He did perfectly. I took quite a few snaps for her to put in her scrapbook and to show off to her friends in Seattle, trying to capture the big crowd with the camera too so they'd be impressed.

All went well till a bee flew up out of the grass right where Growl was going to step, at which point he stopped, then put his front paws on Louanne to pick him up, barking loudly.

She gently pushed his head back to the ground, and he followed her to the end of the course. She came and stood next to me, and I could see her lip tremble.

"That darn bee," she said. "Why did it have to fly up then?"

"Don't worry," I tried to reassure her. "I think the judges also want to see how you do under pressure or with a problem. You handled it very well."

"Really?"

"Really," I said.

"Thanks, Savvy. You always know just the right thing to say." She reached over and held my hand, something she hadn't done for a long time.

On the way home, deep in my heart I felt the whisper of another French phrase, *bien joué.* I smiled at the reassurance. I'd memorized this one, and it had stuck: "Well played. Nicely done."

At the end of the day there was good news and bad news. The good news was that Giggle won a yellow ribbon in the mixed breeds contest. Louanne was thrilled.

The bad news? I found that out in the car on the way home.

"Aunt Maude is coming tomorrow night," Dad said.

"Noooo . . . ! She's going to fix something despicable to eat," I said.

"Now, Savvy, be nice. It's Valentine's Day, so Mom and I are going out to dinner."

"Be nice?"

"Be nice," Dad said.

I thought and thought. And thought. And then I had a brilliant idea. "Maybe we should fix dinner for her," I said innocently.

"Very thoughtful," Dad agreed.

Louanne looked at me and giggled. I held mine back. We'd plan our revenge that very night.

# Chapter 46

On the way home from church, I asked if we could stop at the grocery store to buy a few supplies for our "lovely" dinner with Aunt Maude.

"Savvy, what do you have planned?" Mom asked with a warning tone in her voice.

"Nothing," I said innocently. "I'd like to introduce Aunt Maude to some American food I'm sure she'll like."

Mom pulled over at a large Tesco nearby, and Louanne whipped out the list we'd made the night before. Mom got the cart and soon joined in the swing of things, laughing as we threw items into the cart.

Later that evening Louanne and I were still mixing, chilling, and rolling when Aunt Maude arrived. "Hi, girls. I understand you're making dinner for Auntie tonight?"

"Oh yes," Louanne said. Even Growl seemed to grin. But then maybe it was the excessive belly rub she was giving him.

Mom and Dad came down the stairs. Mom had a beautiful blue dress on and her diamond earrings and necklace.

"I didn't know you owned a tie," I teased my dad.

He smiled but looked kind of embarrassed and earnest, like a kid on a date and not a man over forty. I think he even blushed. He took a rose corsage out of the fridge and pinned it on my mom.

Back home, my friends would be going to the Valentine's dance. While I wasn't sure I'd have been asked, it would have been nice to have at least had a shot at it. Or even received a valentine. But maybe it would have been awful. I could picture it now. Jen had someone to go with. And Samantha surely would have had a lot of guys ask her. In fact, my whole crew would have had dates, and they'd keep waiting for me to tell them that I'd been asked too. When it became clear that I wasn't going to be asked, they'd have started looking at me with sad eyes and talking about their dresses in quiet voices when they thought I couldn't hear them. No, no, better that I was here. At least I had an excuse to be left out.

"Savvy!" My dad's voice broke through my imaginary bubble of trouble. "Are you listening to me? I said we're going."

"Oh, okay, Dad," I said. "Have a great time."

Aunt Maude fussed around in the living room while we finished up dinner. A few minutes later, Louanne announced, "Dinner is served!"

Aunt Maude sat down at the table.

"First, frog-eye salad," I said. "Made through the sacrifice of thousands of tiny little frogs." Actually, it was little round pasta, but who was telling?

"Oh, delicious!" Aunt Maude said. "I hope you got some of the frogs from the back garden. They're so noisy." She dug in and took a big spoonful. Even Louanne, the vegetarian, dug into it. Because, of course, there really was no meat.

"Next," I said, pulling a pan from the oven, "the main course. Pigs in a blanket. For those cold, pork nights."

Aunt Maude gamely picked up a hot dog wrapped in dough and bit into it. She dipped it in ketchup. "Blood?" she asked before taking a bite. Oooh, she was good. I saw Louanne turn white at that.

A few minutes later Louanne came out with dessert. "Dirt pudding," she announced, setting a small bowl of chocolate pudding covered in chocolate cookie crumbs in front of Aunt Maude.

"Tasty!" Aunt Maude said. "And what's this?" She pulled a long, red object from deep inside her pudding.

"A worm, of course," I said. Gummy worms.

We'd tried to beat her at her game, but she beat us anyway. I threw my napkin up as a white flag of surrender. Aunt Maude was too wise to be put off by some crazy food names. She'd won!

Afterward Aunt Maude congratulated us and shockingly invited us to watch some telly with her before we got ready for bed. Aunt Maude never watched telly. We took this as a sign of her approval.

Then I went upstairs and got ready for bed. In the spirit of the holiday, I painted my fingernails red. I could celebrate in some small way, even alone.

# Chapter 47

"Happy Valentine's Day," Jack said as I walked into the newspaper office the next day. He had a flirty twinkle in his eye, and *that smile* was deeper and happier than I'd ever seen it. I was going to answer him, but I had to swallow my gum first, which delayed my response. Good thing. In the second it took me to do that, I saw Melissa come from behind me. He hadn't been talking to me . . . but to her!

"Happy Valentine's Day," she said, giving him a hug. Now friends hug one another from time to time. But everyone can tell the difference between a hug and a *hug*. This was a *hug*. I sighed. I guessed it was time to take Union Jack off my laptop screen saver. Couldn't crush on my friend's boyfriend—just wasn't done.

"Savvy, I have a few questions if you have a minute," Hazelle said.

*For me?* I started toward her. "Sure," I said. "Shoot."

She walked me over to her desk area. As an official staff member, she had her own office space. On a bulletin board were some Peter Chen photos she'd clipped from the Internet, plus some fashion terms from Wikipedia. A big write-up on London Fashion Week, taken from the *Times* of London, lay nearby, listing all the homes, museums, and parks where showings would be held. "According to your knowledge, have I missed anything?" she asked crisply.

I looked it over. "No, not from what I can tell. You've got all the facts down. But you know, the story is more than the facts. You need the human angle."

Hazelle looked up at me. "The human angle?"

"Yes, what makes the story interesting," I said with a little impatience. After all, this had been my story, and I knew—I just knew—I'd have done a better job covering it. I might not have been officially on the WA staff yet, but I'd taken journalism in school back home. I wasn't completely ignorant. "The people, the places, their lives. For example, you might want to talk about the Gorm Strausses and The Beeches and how they interact with Peter Chen. And," I added, "something about Mr. Chen's life, of course."

"I'm not going to simper to the Gorm Strausses," Hazelle said with contempt. "Or carry on about their ancient, snobbish family tree or fancy estate. This is a fashion shoot, Savvy, not a personality piece." With that, she turned back to her work. I noticed she'd started outlining the article. She'd already written her byline—the writer's credit that would run in the paper when the piece itself did.

I turned and headed toward maths. My heart hurt. I wanted that byline. I wanted to write the piece—not only about the fashion, but the people there and how fashion was important to people of all ages and social classes because it allowed them to express themselves. I didn't bother to whine to God about why this had happened, though. I knew why, and I had to take my two lumps with my tea, as my grandmother would say.

In maths my phone went off, alerting me that I had a text message. I felt it vibrate because my book bag was resting against my leg. I put my hand down, slipped my phone out of the bag, and slid it up the side of my leg, all the while hoping Mr. Thompson wasn't looking at me. Brian was. He grinned at me and held out his hand. Oh, that Brian. He was blackmailing me.

"I'll give you some gum later," I promised. He nodded, smiled, and held up his textbook. That blocked Mr. Thompson's view of me, and I could look at my message in peace.

It was from a number I didn't recognize.

Why do you care about Ashley so much? And her house? And her snotty friends? She doesn't care about you.

I looked at Hazelle. She made eye contact with me. It was her! She must have gotten my number from the list in the newspaper office.

I texted my response.

It's not Ashley I care about. It's Penny.

And then a text came flying back at me.

If Penny's so nice, maybe she should make some new friends instead of those lemmings she hangs out with.

I tapped my response. Fastest fingers in the West. Er, in Europe.

Maybe she doesn't want to be your friendship remodeling project.

Well, honestly. It works both ways. I pressed Send and looked at Hazelle. She read the message and then put her phone away without making eye contact again, but she had a hard, unyielding set to her face.

# Chapter 48

The last period of the day, Penny showed me a few sketches she'd made of outfits she thought might fit in with her new style—and a few for me, too. She ripped one out of her notebook. "If you want it," she offered.

"I do! Thanks, Penny."

"Any word on how the Peter Chen fashion shoot article is going to go?" she asked.

I shook my head. "Nothing certain. But I did tell Hazelle that featuring the Gorm Strausses and The Beeches would be an important personal angle to the piece."

"Do you think she'll listen?" Penny asked.

"I hope so," I said with as much cheer as I could muster.

She didn't seem convinced. "My mother is hoping to join Lady Gorm Strauss's garden club this spring when they open it to new members," Penny murmured.

I nodded. Mute.

Before class started, there was a knock on the door, and several year-eleven guys came into the room wearing rugby uniforms. I knew who they were because they'd bought some advert space in last week's paper. They were holding a Valentine's fund-raiser by delivering secret valentines—boxes of chocolates—at the end of the school day. Miss Nodding pursed her lips and allowed the guys to come in and make their announcements. By the look on her face, I suspected that not only did she disapprove of this fund-raiser but she probably hadn't received a secret valentine herself in her century on the planet.

"Well then, we've got four deliveries for this class," said their leader, a tall boy with close-cut black hair and perfectly white, straight teeth. "First, for Elizabeth Mitchell."

Elizabeth raised her hand, and a sweet-looking boy with deep dimples and wavy blond hair walked down the row and handed the box and a gift card to Elizabeth.

"Next, to Hannah Haley."

Hannah raised her hand, and the same boy walked over and handed her a box of chocolates and a card.

"Penny Barrowman," he called out next. Then he said to the guy passing out the chocolates, "I assume you won't need her to raise her hand."

The other boys jostled the dimpled blond, who blushed deeply and made his way down the row to Penny. To my surprise, Penny blushed back as she took the box from him.

I looked at her, my mouth and eyes wide open in surprise. "You . . . him? Him . . . you?"

She nodded and blushed again. I looked at him. I could see it. They were a cute couple. Maybe they'd grow up and have cute little dimpled kids together. Their son would play rugby, and their daughter would like art, or maybe the other way around. And they'd always eat chocolate together every night to remember the romantic beginning to their relationship.

"Savvy!" Penny hissed in my direction. "He has called your name like three times. Raise your hand!"

I snapped out of my reverie and obediently raised my hand, unaware of what and why till the moment they put a large gold box of chocolates in my hand.

"No card," Penny's guy said to me. "Truly anonymous. But . . . it was our most expensive box."

♡

I brought my box of chocolates home and showed it to my parents and to my sister. Dad joked that he was going to have to clean his shotgun now so he'd know how to intimidate the "young man" once we found him.

"But you had to leave your guns in Seattle, Dad," Louanne said innocently. We all got a good laugh out of that. I was thrilled that I'd received the box. But who had sent it?

I knew it wasn't Union Jack. After school on Monday I'd seen Melissa with a box of her own chocolates, and I pretty much knew where she'd gotten them. One of the typesetters for the paper, Alex, had been really nice to me. In fact, he'd invited me to come to school early on Tuesday so he could show me how to set the type. Maybe it was him. I'd pay careful attention to the vibe.

That night I carefully chose the question to answer for this week's Asking for Trouble column. I'd learned my lessons with the other columns lately. I'd had to experience what the people who'd written in had gone through, and I'd learned "their" lesson from Scripture too. This time I was hoping I'd actually learn it for good.

# Chapter 49

Even though I was officially grounded till Sunday the twenty-first, my parents let me go to school early, so on Tuesday I did.

"What are you doing here?" Hazelle asked.

"Thanks for the warm welcome," I said. "Alex is going to show me some stuff with the type-setting program."

"Oh." She turned back to her work.

The typesetting computer was pretty close to Hazelle's desk. As one of the younger, newer members of the paper, she was in the back. I sat next to Alex. "Thanks for showing this to me," I said.

"Nothing at all," he said. "My pleasure." He smiled at me, and I smiled back. It could have been a typical, friendly smile. Or it could have been more.

"Everything is computerized," he said. "So we take the files that the writers give us, and we feed them into this program." He reached one of his newsprint-stained hands across mine and touched a few icons on the touch screen. "Then, in a minute, the document comes up."

And just like that, the article was there in newspaper format. "Cool," I said, breathing out but not in for a while. It was just that exciting.

He grinned. "It's fantastic, isn't it?" He took a piece of newspaper from the large stack of ivory sheets to the side and fed it into the printer. He tinkered around with the typesetter for a minute and pushed a couple more buttons. Soon enough a newspaper draft came out. Most of the page was blank, but there was a dummy article that said, "Peter Chen Charms Wexburg! By Savvy Smith." He handed it to me.

My own name. On a byline. "Thanks, Alex," I said, holding back some tears I didn't know were still there. "But I won't be doing that article."

"What?" he said. "I thought you scooped it for us! I've been seeing advert samples all week from local merchants due to your idea."

"I was going to write it," I explained. "But I . . . well, something came up at home. Hazelle is doing this article now."

"Really? I mean, what came up? This is so important to you."

I hadn't told anyone else. It was kind of embarrassing. A *dog show* rather than a fashion show. But Alex seemed to genuinely care.

"Well, I made a mistake and I got grounded. I had to choose between going to that shoot or taking my little sister to her dog show and doing some photojournalism shots for her. I'd promised her I'd go. So I took her."

"I'm sorry, Savvy," he said, resting his hand kind of close to mine. I didn't move mine closer, but I didn't pull it away, either.

"Me too," I said.

"There'll be another." He looked at the clock. "I'd better get on with the rest of my typesetting."

"Thanks again for showing me."

"Anytime," he said, and he held eye contact for just a second longer than he needed to.

On my way out I glanced at Hazelle. She was absolutely motionless for the first time ever, except for her ears, which were still twitching

from eavesdropping. Her face was flushed red.
She didn't look up as I walked by.

# Chapter 50

In maths a few minutes later, I was trying very hard to concentrate on some equations when I felt my phone buzz in my bag. I ignored it. A minute later it buzzed again.

I reached into my bag, Brian held up his book, and I pulled out my phone. Two messages, both from Hazelle. I'd put her contact information into my phone. It's not like it had been overflowing with friends.

Sit with me at lunch today. I want to talk.

I caught her attention and nodded instead of texting back. After slipping my phone back into my bag, I looked up and saw Mr. Thompson staring at me. Brian started coughing and finally raised his hand to ask for a drink of water. It was nice of him to distract for me.

Then a thought occurred to me. Could he have sent the chocolates?

In PE, Penny stopped me and eyed my slightly frizzy do. "Do you want to use my hair straightener? You know, chic through thick and thin?" She grinned at our inside joke.

I felt sick. This was a major step toward friendship—a friendship I really wanted and enjoyed. "No thanks," I said. "I'm doing a ponytail today."

"Oh, all right . . ." She sounded uncertain.

I tried to smile brightly to indicate that it didn't mean that I didn't want to be good friends. I think she even had capital *B*, capital *F* potential. But until I knew what Hazelle was going to write in her column, I didn't want Penny too closely aligned with me. If Hazelle dropped a bomb, it would be better for Penny not to have been tight with me—the person who'd given the ticket to Hazelle.

At lunch I planned to sit with Hazelle. I waved at Penny and told her I'd text her later, but I think she was a little upset that I wasn't sitting with her.

I'd tell her later that Hazelle had asked. She'd understand. Right?

I sat next to Hazelle, hoping this was important. "So, here I am," I said.

Hazelle opened up her lunch sack and took out a tuna fish sandwich. *Oh, Hazelle,* I thought. *No one eats tuna at school. It smells up the whole room and clings to your clothes for hours after. You might as well have an onion and garlic pie.* But of course, I said nothing.

"Was what you told Alex today the truth?" she asked.

"I always tell the truth," I said. Well, almost always. Say, 99 percent of the time. And I come clean later if I don't.

"You gave up doing the article to take your sister to a dog show?"

"Listen, Hazelle, this was really hard for me, so please don't make fun of me, okay?"

She took another bite of tuna. "I'm not making fun of you," she said after swallowing. "I'm just . . . surprised. You know my older sister, Julia, used to be the editor of the WA *Times,* right?"

I nodded. Her sister and Union Jack were the two people who had chosen the secret columnist last December from among the dozens of people vying for it, including Hazelle and, of course, me. No one except Julia, Jack, and me knew that I was the column's author.

"I always admired my big sister. But she would never have picked a dog show—or me—over her writing. She has principles. Which is good, but . . ." She set down her sandwich and looked as if she might cry. "Kindness to your sister is a good principle too. I don't think I understood you very well, Savvy. I'm sorry."

And then I understood. I looked at Hazelle, and instead of seeing frizzy brown hair and red lipstick, I saw Louanne, a little sister who was wonderful and smart and loving and wanted some of her sister's time. But Hazelle's sister had none to offer.

"I admire *your* principles. You don't let anyone change who you are."

"My sister has never taken time to help me, really," Hazelle said. "She didn't pick me for the Asking for Trouble column, of course. I'm not sure who she picked. Someone who's a year twelve, I suppose. I guess she had to be fair."

I vowed right then that I would not divulge my secret to anyone, if only to save Hazelle's broken heart. What would she think and feel if she knew it was me?

I took a bite of my cheese and tomato sandwich. I felt, more than saw, the Aristocats staring at me sitting with weepy Hazelle.

"I have asked her to critique my work before," Hazelle continued. "She has done it a time or two, but she's so busy now."

"Well, I really admire the fact that you get edited," I said. "You let your sister and Jack and Melissa and the other paper staff edit and comment on your work. That takes guts."

She crumpled a piece of paper towel inside her lunch bag and smiled. "You said you always tell the truth, right?"

I gulped. Uh-oh. "Yes."

"Would you read the novel I'm writing? I'd like your opinion on it."

"Mine?" I could barely contain my shock.

"Yours," she said. "And don't hold back. No matter what happens, friends or no, the main thing is to be completely honest in the stuff you write and in the critique you offer. No polish. No varnish. No prettying things up. That's what my sister always says. So let me know what you think."

"Okay." I wondered if she was telling me that

about her own piece or if she was trying to send me a message about what to expect from her Peter Chen piece. "What kind of novel is it?"

"A romance," she said. "When are you done being grounded?"

"Sunday. The day after the shoot."

"I'll bring my novel sometime this week," she said. "And remember—I want the truth."

"Okay," I said. Oh, dear. What if I hated it?

# Chapter 51

On Thursday I woke up early. "Dad, can you help me with this?" I asked, holding out my Au Revoir bag.

He sat at the kitchen table reading the *Times* and chugging his morning tomato juice. "Whatcha need, Sav?" he asked.

I stuck my hand through the bottom of the bag and waved at him. "I don't think this is going to hold any newspapers."

He grinned, opened up the junk drawer, and pulled out a roll of duct tape. "This oughta do it."

I grimaced. "Okay. Just don't put any where it can be seen from the outside."

Now that my bag was held together, I shook Growl off my leg and headed to school. The newspaper office was abuzz with energy as it was every Thursday. Usually Hazelle helped me load the bags, but she was busy preparing for the Peter Chen shoot, only two days away. I started slipping that day's paper into my wounded delivery bag.

"Here, let me help you with that." Alex hopped off of the table he'd been sitting at, chatting with Rodney, and headed over to the stacks of paper.

"Thanks very much," I said, surprising myself as I heard the British phrase come out of my American mouth.

"Nothing at all," he reassured me with a grin. "Anytime, actually."

I smiled back at him but without any signal of commitment or affection. He was nice.

After delivering the papers, I checked my cell phone to see what time it was. My phone background was the verse I'd based this week's Asking for Trouble response on, Galatians 6:9. I'd typed it in earlier this week to encourage myself every time I looked at my phone: "Let's not get tired of doing what is good. At just the right time we will reap a harvest of blessing if we don't give up."

Maybe I had time to read the column before class. As I did, I hoped that my own advice would pay off. Not just for the person who wrote in and not just for me. But for Penny, who had done nice things that I hoped would be paid back with good and not evil.

**D**ear Asking for Trouble, Okay, so there's this sports team I've wanted to join. I won't say which one because then everyone will know who's writing this. Anyway, I practice every day after school, have taken a few private lessons, and run to keep in good condition. But I still haven't earned a spot on the team. Meanwhile, the coach's kid, who can't play worth pence, is still on the starting lineup. The assistant coach says my turn is coming, and it's my dream to play on the team, but it doesn't seem to be working out. Should I quit?

Sincerely,
*Wants to Play*

♡

**D**ear Play, You're doing all the right things. You're working hard and keeping at it. The assistant coach says your time is coming, and he or she should know

... right? A dream isn't something to throw away lightly just because things are getting tough. Hang in there, because the truth of the matter is, if you keep on doing what's right, what's good, sooner or later (sooner, I hope!) it's going to pay off. Then you'll have earned not only a spot on the team but also the respect of your teammates. Good things are coming.

Hang in there,
*Asking for Trouble*

# Chapter 52

The next day, Friday, was dress-down day. I wore one of my bohemian fashionista outfits, and Penny, I was proud to notice, wore a pair of color-washed jeans with a soft cashmere sweater. I had never seen an Aristocat in color-washed jeans.

I approached the lunch table slowly, trying to juggle a copy of Hazelle's manuscript, which she'd just handed to me, my book bag, and my lunch. As I got closer, I overheard Ashley talking to Penny.

"It's a fashion shoot, not a farming convention," she said. "You asked me for tickets for Savvy—not Hazelle. I wouldn't have given them to you had I known. Mum isn't happy either."

I saw Hazelle's ears quiver at the next table. She had heard too.

Penny's voice was soft but firm. "It's not like she can jolly well tell the editor who to send on the shoot," Penny said. "She told me that he assigned Hazelle." That was technically true, since Jack had promised Hazelle to come with me. Penny didn't mention the grounding, though.

Ashley grunted. "I suppose not," she said. "But tomorrow's shoot had better be as smooth as butter and cream, and the Wexburg Academy write-up had better be glowing."

I got close to the table, and they stopped talking.

"Can I sit here?" I asked. Penny scooted over. Ashley got up and left.

Penny took my lunch bag and the stack of papers from my hands. "What's this?" she asked.

"Oh . . . some reading." Hazelle hadn't said I could mention her novel to anyone else. So I wouldn't.

♥

In composition class Mrs. Beasley handed my paper back in front of the whole class. "Fantastic work, Miss Smith," she said. "Best I've seen in a long time."

I smiled and held out my hand as she put the essay into it. But then she had to go and ruin the whole thing.

"Someday," she said, "maybe you'll do more on the school newspaper than deliver them."

I heard a sarcastic little cough and throat clearing. I didn't need to turn my head to know who it was. Ashley. If I'd been a less kind person, I'd ask her if she was coughing up a hairball. I half wished that Hazelle would notice a broken-down bathroom or crazy valet at The Beeches and mention it in her article. Kidding!

Of course, I couldn't tell Mrs. Beasley, the class, or anyone else that I was the author of Asking for Trouble. Even Ashley read the advice column. Penny had told me.

Well, I take that back. I *could* tell that I was the author. But I'd said I wouldn't. And now I had even more reason to keep it a secret. It would really hurt Hazelle if she knew that her sister had chosen me, a new writer, over her.

I hope she paid my loyalty back with some loyalty of her own when it came time to write the article. But she'd made it pretty clear that she'd write what she wanted.

*Dear Jesus, let this turn out well.*

# Chapter 53

Saturday morning, the morning of the Peter Chen shoot, I got up early. I put on the white knit skirt, the leggings, the chunky brown shoes, and even some lip gloss and eye makeup. I wanted to see what I would have looked like for the shoot. I wanted to see the outfit on, and I hadn't put it on since my trip with Mom to Topshop.

A knock came on the door.

"Um, uh, hang on a minute. Who is it?"

"Mom."

"I'm changing." I whipped off the outfit, put my pj's back on, and tossed on my robe. "Come on in," I said.

She walked in. "Just get up?"

"Why?" I asked.

"Since when do you go to bed with makeup on? fresh makeup?"

I sighed. "I was trying on the outfit I was going to wear today," I said. "For kicks."

She leaned over and hugged me. "You made a bad decision followed by a good decision. That's the right order."

I leaned into her hug and squeezed back some tears. "I know," I muffled into her robe. "Will you drive me by The Beeches later?" I asked. "Not to go in, of course. Just to look."

"Are you sure you want to do that?"

I nodded.

"Okay, then," Mom said. "But first, I think someone has a present for you."

I heard the dog race up the stairs, followed shortly by the padding of Louanne's slippered feet.

"Chocolate chip pancakes," she said. "I made them myself."

♡

Later that afternoon we drove by Ashley's house. There were three long limos in the driveway. I could hear the pump of rock music coming from inside the house, and I saw a huge batch of lights

and props in the garden. There must be an outdoor shoot too.

I saw something that surprised me a little.
Penny's mother's car was there. I hadn't known
that Penny was going too. I wondered if she was
inside with Hazelle.

# Chapter 54

The next morning we went to church. On the way there my dad said, "If you want to sign up for Wednesday nights, we can come from now on."

I nodded. "Okay. Maybe. We'll see." I made a deal with God. If someone talked to me during Sunday school, I'd go on Wednesday. If not, I wouldn't. I didn't really expect to go, frankly. I was growing tired of doing good and not reaping the promised harvest of blessing.

After church I walked boldly into the class. I knew no one was going to talk with me—they hadn't last week, either. The class started. No one sat next to me. I felt smug. *See? It's not working.*

I stood up to sing the worship song and closed my eyes and raised my hands. When I opened my eyes, Supriya was next to me.

"Hi, Savvy," she said. I was pleased and surprised that she was there and that she remembered my name.

"Hi, Supriya," I said.

She grinned. I think she was happy that I'd remembered her name too. I loved her nose stud and her sari. Hmm. Maybe I should change my fashion to chic East Indian. Okay, not really.

But it did look supercute on her.

"You should come on Wednesdays," she said as we settled down for the DVD they were preparing to show. "We won't meet again for a couple of weeks, till after the term break. But I'll see you then?"

"Yes," I said. After all, a deal was a deal.

After church we drove home, and my parents went to take their nap. I did some homework and wondered if I should call or text someone and ask how the shoot went. Not Hazelle. She'd think I was being nosy. Penny.

I texted her.

How did the Peter Chen shoot go?

I waited for a bit but heard nothing back. I made sure I'd punched in the right number—ones and not sevens. Yep.

I did some more homework, then cut pictures out of the latest edition of *Teen Vogue*. I made a banner for my laptop that said *My Heroes Don't Wear Size Zeroes*. I checked the phone again. Nothing. I hoped things had gone well.

A knock came on my bedroom door. It flew open before I even had a chance to say anything. Definitely against house rules.

"Savvy! There's a package for you. It was at the front door." Louanne held it in her hands. "I knew you wouldn't mind if I brought it in."

"Hand it to me!" This was my second secret package this month!

# Chapter 55

I unwrapped the brown paper and threw it on the floor. Growl raced over and started chewing and dragging the paper around the room, but I didn't care. I opened the box and lifted out . . .

"A new designer bag!" I leaped off the bed and danced around the room. It was at least as big as my Au Revoir bag. Neon green with big modernist swirls. A catchy little handle, totally stylish. I didn't know who the designer was, but I'd find out.

"Is there a note inside?" Louanne asked.

I opened it up. It was cavernous inside, but I couldn't see a note or a card. Nothing. I stuck my whole head in the bag and breathed in that new-leather scent. Wow. The paper was going to be delivered in style now, and just in time. The Au Revoir was falling apart.

"Who sent it?" Louanne said. "Do you know?"

"Nope."

"Do you think it was your secret valentine?" she asked.

I laughed out loud. "I don't know any guy my age who could pick out this bag or who would even think of it." I was so happy I had to celebrate. "You hungry?" I asked her.

She nodded. "Sure. Why?"

"I still haven't taken you to Fishcoteque for your birthday. We can tell Mom and Dad that we're going now. I'm officially off grounding."

"Yes!" Now Louanne danced around the room, and Growl, getting in the mood of things, ran up and down the hallway, barking.

A few minutes later Louanne and I strolled into the steamy comfort of the fish-and-chips shop. The place was packed, it being Sunday and all.

"Company today, eh? Not like that boy you brought last month," Jeannie said to me, and Louanne gave me a sly smile. I elbowed her.

"Mushy peas and chips?" she asked.

"No, I'm not a vegan anymore. The usual for

me. But mushy peas and chips for my sister . . . and two Fantas."

"That's what it'll be, then," she said. "Seven pounds even."

I paid her with a ten-pound note and decided to slip the change into the one and only tiny compartment stitched into the side of my new designer bag. I reached my fingers in, undid the Velcro, and went to slip the note in.

Wait. Something was already in the pocket. A British flag coin purse. I reached my thumb and forefinger in and pulled it out. Then I unclasped the purse. One lone object floated inside. A coin.

"One p," I said, withdrawing it. I looked at it. On one side was a picture of Queen Elizabeth. On the other were the words *ONE PENNY* in big, bold type. That's right—a pence was known as p, but also as a penny!

"Penny," I whispered. It was a silent message. Late that night I got a text from her.

Shoot went fine. Hazelle spoke to no one. See you in school tomorrow.

# Chapter 56

Monday. The day went by okay. In maths I asked Hazelle how the Peter Chen shoot went and she said fine, she got everything she needed for the article. Brian snapped his gum and got detention, and then he handed the remaining sticks to me, saying it was for safekeeping and he'd get it from me later. Hmm. Didn't know what to make of that.

Penny asked me at lunch if Hazelle had given any indication of what she was writing about. I shook my head. I mentioned my wonderful new designer bag and how much I loved it. Penny made a polite comment but offered no hint that she'd given it to me. Should I have pushed the subject?

Tuesday. The newspaper office was humming. All articles were due that day. I stopped by and cleaned up a bit but couldn't see what anyone was writing or editing without being a completely nosy creeper and staring over their shoulders. Went home wondering.

Wednesday. There was no church tonight—the next meeting would be in two weeks. Growl ripped up the one-pound notes left over from Fishcoteque. Louanne said she's sorry. Mom said I should keep my money in a safe place. I retreated to my room to steam in private.

Tomorrow the paper would be out.

# Chapter 57

I got to school early the next morning—psyched, I must say, to have retired the dear old Au Revoir and start using my fabulous lime green designer bag. I'd looked it up online. It was a Peter Chen and worth nearly $500 (by my American dollar calculations). Even Penny wouldn't have spent that much. Had I been wrong about who the giver had been? But who else would have done it?

The newsroom was busy as everyone finished up last-minute details. I'd expected Hazelle to gloat over her first full-bylined article. I figured she'd have a copy of it cut out and hanging on the bulletin board over her desk or something. But nothing. In fact, she just made small talk with me as she loaded the papers into the bag. I chitchatted back. I was dying to open the paper and read it but didn't want to seem too "eager beaver."

I walked as fast as I could without looking like a geek and put the papers into the paper holders around the school. Then I took a seat on a bench outside the gym and opened the paper. I carefully scanned each of the six pages. Nothing. I mean, the usuals. Rodney's sports article. The luncheon menu. An article about A-level exams. A small local piece about a new shop opening in town. Adverts. Nothing at all about Peter Chen and the fashion shoot.

Had they killed the article? Had they decided not to do it at all? That might even be worse than nothing at all from Ashley's point of view, and therefore worse for Penny. A sick, unsettled feeling rose in my gut and then seeped out, in the form of sweat, through my pores.

I went to maths and made it there just before the bell. "Cover for me, okay?" I whispered to Brian. He dutifully held up his book while I texted Hazelle.

No Peter Chen article?

I held on to my phone, hoping Mr. Thompson wouldn't come down the row and confiscate it, hoping Hazelle would risk reading and then answering a text in class again. But her phone must have been turned off, because she didn't even look at me. After a few minutes, Brian put his book back down and we got to work.

After class I quickly packed up so I could stop Hazelle before she left for her second period.

"Hazelle," I said. "Can I talk with you for a minute?"

She stopped. "Sure. What do you need?"

"Well, I was wondering . . . I didn't see the Peter Chen article in the paper. I was wondering . . . did you kill it? Did Jack?"

She laughed. "No, Savvy, it's not killed. I just decided to delay it for a week so I could do a little fill-in information with the London Fashion Week and run a sidebar of that next to my article."

Was I imagining things, or had she emphasized the *my* in that sentence?

"It'll run next week," she said, smiling. "Oh . . . did you get a chance to read my novel yet?"

Uh-oh. I mean, I'd started, but then I got carried away with other things, and honestly I'd simply forgotten about it. "I'm sorry; I haven't finished it," I said. "I want to give it my full concentration. I'll finish it this week. I promise."

"No problem," she said. "I'm looking forward to your honest opinion." Then she hurried to her second period, and I hurried to PE.

As I suspected, *they* were waiting for me in PE.

"No article about The Beeches in today's paper." Ashley said this; she didn't ask it. And I noticed that the article had now gone, in her mind, from one about Peter Chen to one about The Beeches.

"Hazelle just told me that she's writing it up next week so she can partner it with some information about the world-famous London Fashion Week," I said. "Which will make it a bigger deal."

"Jolly," Ashley said, and she seemed satisfied.

I looked at Penny. The pink started coming back into her pale face.

# Chapter 58

After school I collected the leftover newspapers as usual, though there weren't many to collect. Then I brought them back to the newspaper office. As I walked into the room, I thought I saw Jack kiss Melissa before disappearing into his office, but I couldn't be sure. Of course, the slight flush on her face when she saw me could have been a clue that it had happened.

I set down the papers and walked by the wall with little cubbies, one for each staff member. I glanced at the one with my name on it and walked on. Then I stopped, backed up, and looked again. There was something in my box. An envelope.

Sixteen2TwentyOne
CATWALK
FASHION
SHOW

Saturday, February 27,
@ 2 o'clock in the afternoon

BRITISH MUSEUM
Great Russell Street, London

Tickets to a London Fashion Week show? An actual show in London, not a shoot—as cool as that may be—in Wexburg? With real models? the paparazzi? I turned around. The only other person in the room was Melissa, her head down over an advertisement she was laying out for next week's paper.

"Melissa." I walked toward her holding the tickets in my hand. "These were in my box for Saturday . . . do you know who put them in there?"

She looked them over. "Wow, Savvy! Brilliant!"

Then she handed them back to me. "I can't say that I know who put them in there. I didn't see. But . . . you do know that Hazelle's dad is a security guard at the British Museum, right? Good sleuthing might suggest that possibly . . ."

I stared at the tickets. "I-I should ask her to come with me."

Melissa gave me a wry look. "Savvy, does the catwalk seem like something she'd want to go to?"

I giggled. "Uh, no. She told me herself she hated fashion."

Melissa nodded. "And one expects that if she wanted a ticket for herself she could have gotten one."

"Well, I should at least thank her," I said. My mother raised me with good manners.

Melissa pulled me into the chair next to her. "So, Savvy, here's something to know about British people. We don't like the spotlight, for the most part. It embarrasses us to be recognized for doing something. We'd much rather go about our business, not make a fuss, and be glad to have done some good." She motioned to a copy of the latest newspaper, which was thrown on her desk.

"For example, that's what makes the Asking for Trouble column so successful."

Inside I grinned, though I didn't twitch a muscle on the outside. I was more British than I knew. And it was clear—kiss or no kiss—that Jack hadn't spilled our secret even to his girlfriend. But the attitude certainly explained Penny's gift of the bag. And even Father Christmas.

"So you don't think I should say anything to her?"

"Nope. Take a couple of good snaps of the event that she can run alongside her article. She'll like that."

I nodded and packed up to leave. Well, who would have guessed? Hazelle. I thought about the Aristocats snubbing her and her security guard dad. Better to be a security guard, I thought, than an insecurity guard, which was what most of their clique was.

And then I thought about Penny and felt convicted. It was just better not to make assumptions about anyone. Judge a tree by its fruit, Jesus had said.

Later that night, after my parents had said I could go to the show, I grabbed my phone to text Penny to see if she could come too.

She wrote back:

Love to. How'd you get the tickets?

I couldn't tell her, though I wished I could give Hazelle credit where it was due. I also wished I knew if this meant that the article in the WA *Times* would go the way I wanted it to. But truly I had no idea. I'd given up on second-guessing Hazelle.

# Chapter 59

"I'm really excited," Penny said as she climbed into our car. I wondered if she'd be embarrassed to ride in our normal used car instead of her mom's zippy sports car. But she gave no indication that she felt that way at all. "It's been ages since I've been to a London fashion show, really. And nothing as exciting as Sixteen2TwentyOne. Thanks for inviting me!"

"It's nothing at all," I said, trying hard to show that British modesty. But then my American enthusiasm burst out. "There's no one I'd rather take," I told her, and she grinned. *Thank You, God, for a good friend.* And for these tickets! I didn't let on to Penny that I'd never been to a fashion show.

She and I chatted all the way into London, but as we grew closer, the car got quieter. I stared out the window, watching the shiny black London taxis streak by. The constant London rain meant that dozens of beautifully colored umbrellas—uh, brollies—seemed to sprout from the slick pavement like spring flowers, blossoming over and hiding the people who sheltered under them. My dad dropped us off in front of the museum. There were tons of limos, little swarms of paparazzi buzzing around, and smartly dressed people with smooth skin and flawless makeup.

I smoothed my white knit skirt, glad for the chunky heels on the brown shoes, which would make me a bit taller today instead of a shrub among all these willows.

"I'm going to tour the Imperial War Museum. Text me when you're ready to leave," Dad said.

I promised I would, and then Penny and I got out of the car. I'd brought my Peter Chen bag for a pop of color, and although she'd said nothing, I noticed that Penny smiled when she saw me carrying it.

We walked up the dozens of stairs toward the large building, which was held up by imposing concrete colonnades that had been sculpted a century or more ago. We walked past the general crowds and into the great central chamber made of marble, as cold and sleek and refined as the Aristocats. Well, that wasn't fair. Penny wasn't cold.

I wondered where the show was being held. "I hope it's not with the Egyptian art," I said.

"Why not?" Penny asked, motioning toward a sign and a crowd of well-dressed women.

"Mummies creep me out," I said.

"Well, they knew how to do their eye makeup," she teased and nudged me toward the crowd. Sure enough, it was the right direction.

"Tickets, please." Even the ticket taker was dressed in a HUGO BOSS suit. Smooth! He led us to our seats, which were about three-fourths of the way back, and handed us a bag.

"What's this?" I asked Penny.

"Goody bag," she said. "They hand them out at all the fashion shows. Well, not the Peter Chen one at Ashley's. They did have a table full of extremely nice giveaways at the back, though. Samples and makeup and . . . bags and such," she said.

Aha! Now I knew where the bag came from. "I'm sorry I missed it," I said. "What did Hazelle take?"

"I don't know. I got there early because I'm Ashley's friend, and we got to pick the best things. By the time the others arrived, we were seated."

The music started then, and after the introduction the girls started strutting down the catwalk. All of them had extremely poufy, crimped hair, sticking way out from their heads.

"Savvy, look, they're copying your first-day-back-after-holidays hairstyle," Penny whispered, and we both laughed out loud.

I got my phone out to take a few snaps—it had a great camera attached. I looked at the screen. Galatians 6:9 flashed across it still.

I grinned. The truth is always the truth.

I took a few pictures of some of the runway models, including one wearing thin leggings with faint stars on them and a denim skirt that I thought was completely cute. I held the camera back from myself and took one of me too. Then I took one of Penny, who looked great. "New outfit?"

"Mmm-hmm. To go with my new style," she said. It felt good. I hadn't been able to give her anything like a Peter Chen bag. But I'd given her the confidence to try something new.

"You took a lot of pictures," she said on the way out.

"Hazelle wants one or two to go along with the article she's writing," I said. It was to be a two-page spread. Even Asking for Trouble would be bumped a week. A tiny part of me still envied her the byline. But I'd keep wrestling with it.

"Hmm," Penny said, nodding. "It's coming out next week?"

"Yes."

# Chapter 60

There was no school on Monday—bank holiday—
which made Tuesday an even busier day. I walked
into the newspaper office before school although
I didn't have any articles that week. I'd already
e-mailed Hazelle the pictures I'd taken at the
photo shoot.

I walked up behind her. "How was your
weekend?"

"Busy," she said. "Finishing up this piece." I
could see that she was working on her article,
but she minimized the screen when I approached
her—no doubt so I couldn't see what was on it.
Well, I couldn't blame her. The ice had broken on
our relationship, but it's not like we were swim-
ming in the warm pool of friendship yet.

"Can I help?" I asked.

And to my surprise, she said, "Yes. I know that you have some photojournalism experience, even if you're new to writing. I need to choose a picture to run alongside the piece." She paged through a half dozen, some that I'd taken from the London show at the museum and some that she'd taken at the Peter Chen shoot. The one on top was of Ashley. Oh, how Ashley would love it if her picture were in the paper. All would be well if it were chosen.

I thumbed through the photos for a few minutes. Then I tapped one. "This one, I think. No, I'm sure. This one."

Hazelle didn't comment right away—she just pulled the picture to her. Finally she said, "Okay." Then she looked up at me.

"Wow! Your new lipstick is great!" The words burst out before I could gate them. I prepared myself for a blast from the furnace. But that's not what I got.

"Do you think so?" she asked, almost shyly. "I took it from the giveaway table at the Peter Chen shoot."

"It's fantastic," I said with meaning. "You picked just the right color. You've got a knack you didn't know about."

"Thank you, Savvy," she said. She pushed her hair behind her ears and turned to her computer. "I'd better get back to work." She reasserted her brusque, controlled voice. "This is due by the end of the day."

Then it hit me. I'd forgotten to finish reading Hazelle's manuscript and let her know what I honestly thought. I'd do it right after school.

# Chapter 61

Hi, Hazelle,

Thanks for letting me read your book. I have to say—
I'm really impressed. I'm dying to know if Anthony
really changed his mind about Emily or if he's just
playing hard to get. I hope she doesn't fall for it.
He's a player. She'd be much better off with Rick.
I marked a few things on the manuscript (I'll bring it
to class) just FYI. But I think it's great work.

Savvy

E-mail, from Hazelle, to me. Two hours later:

Savvy,

Thanks for taking the time to read this. It means
a lot to me. I'm glad you liked it but also glad

you marked a few places where I can use some improvement. See you tomorrow.

Hazelle

I could only hope she wouldn't use the school paper to point out, honestly, where the Gorm Strausses needed improvement.

# Chapter 62

I could barely sleep on Wednesday night, and I got to school early on Thursday. I didn't even eat breakfast, although my mom had made waffles with golden syrup, which I love.

The office was buzzing when I arrived, and Hazelle was the center of attention. Everyone was congratulating her—her first big piece, a two-page spread, and it looked great. Her article had pulled in the most money in advertising dollars of any we'd done yet. The village stores wanted girls to know that they could buy fashionable clothes and accessories right there in town.

Well, thankfully I hadn't gotten the ads or written the article, so my honesty wasn't compromised. Ha!

I congratulated Hazelle and then began to load the papers into my bag. I planned to read it myself after delivering them, just in case I didn't like what had been written.

"Here, let me help." Alex left the crowd and held the Peter Chen bag open so I could slide the papers in.

"Thanks very much," I said. My second British response this month!

"Not at all," he said. He lowered his voice. "Part of this celebration is yours, you know, Savvy."

I shrugged. "Hazelle worked very hard."

"She did," he said. "But she couldn't have done it without you. You're good at keeping a low profile." He held my gaze for a minute before grinning and looking away.

Wow. That had been personal. Did he . . . like me? Or did he know my Asking for Trouble secret? He did the paper layout, after all.

I took the papers in my new delivery bag and started stocking the distribution centers. The paper holder by the gym was the last one I stocked.

"Have an extra?"

I looked up. It was Tommy.

"I do." I handed one to him.

"Got anything you've written in there?" he asked. The group of friends he'd walked in with were starting to look antsy.

"Not this week," I said. "But soon."

"Let me know when you do," he said, and then he smiled. You know, his smile was even more *that smile* than Jack's. Funny, I hadn't noticed before.

He waved good-bye and headed off with his impatient friends. I sat down on the bench to scan the article.

It was really well written, I had to admit. Hazelle had done her homework—she knew all about Peter Chen and the models' names, and she interwove that with the fashion concerns of the girls at Wexburg Academy. She didn't gush about Ashley, but she did call The Beeches "a rich, historic venue perfectly suited to high fashion" and mentioned the Gorm Strauss family as "local aristocracy long given to public service." Well, she'd kept it to the facts, as she'd said she would, but she'd found facts that would please Ashley—and protect Penny. My sigh of relief was like a slowly draining balloon. And then, best of all, the picture.

Penny. I wondered if Ashley would be angry that it wasn't her. I'd find out in PE.

# Chapter 63

In PE everyone congratulated Penny. And they congratulated Ashley too because, well, they wanted to feed the bear and not poke the bear. I could understand that.

Only Gwennie noticed my name in tiny, teeny font under the photo, with the copyright mark. "Congratulations on the photo," she said. "It's a start!"

"It's a start," I agreed and suited up.

Penny had been put on another floor hockey team, but she came over and gave me a quick hug.

"Can I use your straightener after class?" I asked, hoping she'd know what I was *really* saying. "Chic through thick and thin?"

She grinned. "Of course." She started to walk away. "*Friends* through thick and thin. Right, Savvy?"

She got the message. "Right!" I grinned as we jogged toward the gym.

That afternoon at home, I had a few important things to do:

1. Put away the stash of fashion mags I'd used for Operation Help Hazelle in a Hurry.

It had taken me long enough, but I'd finally gotten the message that it was okay to look good on the outside, but if I took care of who I was on the inside, that light would shine through and be bright enough for others to decide if they, too, wanted an inside remodel job. And oh, uh, I could leave that work to them, and to the Holy Spirit.

2. Take Jack's picture off my laptop screen saver.

He was my friend's boyfriend now, and it was the right thing to do. It looked awfully empty on there, just the flying computer logo screen saver. It had displayed a crush's picture on it for, I don't know, a year?

3. Clean off my dresser.

Which I did. But I left one thing . . . my gold chocolate candy box from my secret admirer. My heart skipped a beat. I knew who I wanted it to be.

These Brits were very good at keeping secrets. And I understood. I was getting pretty good at it myself.

Only now I was getting better at figuring them out too. *Beware, anonymous candy giver,* I thought as I opened a pack of Smarties and popped a few into my mouth. *Beware!*

Your Father, who sees what is done in secret, will reward you.   Matthew 6:4, NIV

# for GIRLS Only! DEVOTIONS

**For Girls Only!**
This devotional gets right to the heart of many topics you face:

- feeling like you don't measure up
- dealing with gossip
- trying to face your fears

Through Bible verses, stories about real issues, and self-quizzes, this devotional is a fun way to learn more about living out your faith in real life.

Filled with cool sketches and easy-to-understand devotions, *For Girls Only!* is a great tool for spending time with God and finding out more about yourself!

For more information, visit www.tyndale.com/kids.

CP0388